RAMSAY
Dealer of Death

Gerard Denza

This book is dedicated to:
James Denza and Phil Strumolo
with many thanks.

TABLE OF CONTENTS

GODS, GODDESSES, AND MORTALS

Ramsay Francesca Cruz-Bast: a young and beautiful woman who is tricked into marrying the leader of an occult group. Her instinct is to rebel against fate and destiny.

Maria Cruz: Ramsay's sister, who is baffled by her sister's marriage to a strange man who no one in the family has met.

Francesca Ramirez: Ramsay's aunt who is a member of an occult group. She is the one who arranges Ramsay's marriage.

Dr. Jeffrey Bast: Ramsay's husband and a man who may be as old as the pyramids. He is also a cold-blooded killer.

Osiris: a white, sphinx cat.

Lisa Dunkirk: a not so rich woman and a snob.

Timothy Fields: a British aristocrat who is not as brave as everyone thinks he is.

Allyson Hendricks: a former figure skater and the undisputed beauty of the group.

Kenjiro Kaziyama: a black belt warrior who re-defines the word bravery. It is he who presents Ramsay with the "tools" of death.

Armando Castaneda: a man who is given to cynicism. He is devoted to Dr. Bast.

Marcus: a quiet, but strong man who was severely burnt during a sacred ritual.

Tana: a woman with interesting dreams and manners.

Julietta Tebaldi: a living "mannequin" who has lived since the dawn of Man.

Carmino: an enemy or a friend? Ramsay and he form an unholy alliance.

Renso: a priest who is a member of his own evil brotherhood.

BOOK I
RAMSAY

CHAPTER I
THE BUS RIDE

THE BUS driver was silent and so was everyone else in that vehicle which penetrated its way through the darkness and rain. I was sitting in the center of the bus not quite opposite the exit door. Directly behind me was someone steeped in shadows...a woman, I think. Her presence gave me no comfort at all. I don't derive comfort from other women. Men are my comfort, a spiritual comfort, if you would. Opposite the woman was a young man of about twenty. His blonde hair was cut short, as if not so long ago he had been bald. I didn't like his look or the confused expression on his face. He kept avoiding my glances as though he were frightened of me. I hate stupidity, particularly in a man.

None of us were getting off the bus, at least not yet, and no new passengers were getting on. The bus driver was having difficulty navigating through the downpour. The windshield wipers could barely keep off the nearly solid sheets of rain. It felt to me that the rain had chosen this bus as a sacrificial object to be punished and cleansed and destroyed in the process.

A sacrament, as I was to learn, could be cruel.

I should introduce myself to you. My name is Ramsay Francesca Cruz. I am Spanish by birth and upbringing and I am now on my way to see my sister, Maria. And, quite frankly, I must be out of my mind to travel in such terrible weather. But, my sister and I are closer to each other now than we have ever been, for our entire family is deceased.

Looking out the rain splattered window, I can see nothing at all...except my own distorted reflection of a woman who is discontent with herself and life. There are fine lines around my eyes and forehead and, in a strange way, they add to that classic beauty which my sister says that I possess. Quite by reflex, I touch my black hair which has been recently cut to just an inch or so above my shoulders. I had just a trace of a perm put into it to give it that "lift" which I feel my face now needs.

On the seat next to me is my black, overnight bag. I patted it with my gloved hand; a gesture which gives me comfort. My beautiful black, patent leather purse is on my lap. It was a birthday present from a beloved aunt who I think of every day. I take out the lipstick and compact for a tiny repair job. My lipstick, another present from Aunt Francesca, is a black enameled case with tiny crystal studs about its length. The lipstick is my favorite shade of red. Carefully, I apply the make-up.

My stop has to be soon. And, would this rain never end or at least diminish? The sheets of rain keep pounding like cannon shots. If I don't get off soon, it will drive me quite mad.

Finally, the bus slows down and I can see the glass shelter. I'm relieved to see that vandals haven't demolished it. Perhaps, I would even be safe until my sister came for me.

I'm smiling. I'm in love. After so many years, I've met the man whom I knew so long ago. His name is Mark. But, I must not think of him now. Later, I will think of him when I go to bed so that I may dream of him and feel him close to me...to feel him within me and touching me and hurting me with sweet pleasure. And, I will drive him mad, of course, as a woman should. These thoughts must come later because soon Maria will be here and I don't want her to suspect anything just yet. One must give only subtle hints about such thoughts in order to leave the other person hungering for more intimate and revealing details.

The light within this shelter was the only light in the world at that moment. Was I truly alone in the darkness and the rain? I wasn't. I could hear the footfall even though there was no sound to give it away. Its approach disturbed the air that it displaced...the air that it pushed away was pushed toward me. It was coming for me.

I picked up my overnight bag and fled into the night. Immediately, I was drenched, but the sound of my high heels hitting the pavement gave me reassurance. I could move and breathe and my presence was real and could be heard. I was alone in this darkness, but not frightened. Yet, what propelled me to flee from the imagined safety of the bus shelter? I knew what it was. I didn't want to see the face of my pursuer for it would reveal too much for me. Too many questions would be answered and for this I want Mark with me. Together, we would come to terms with whatever we had to.

That thing was catching up to me. Just a few more steps and I'd be at my sister's house. I ran the distance with my free arm swaying to and fro in a frantic motion. My pursuer was getting closer.

At last, I reached my destination. I banged on the door to be let in. I closed my eyes tightly and screamed out my sister's name.

It's upon me now.

I screamed.

-But is my sister crazy or is she just taking leave of her senses? Why are you screaming? What are you so afraid of?

I stumbled a step or two backward but managed not to fall. My overnight bag dropped into the hallway as I clutched my purse tightly to my side. Maria closed the door, but only after a hesitation for she, too, felt that presence. She looked to her left and, then, to her right just as Moses did after he killed the Egyptian soldier. It was a look into his past and into his future. But, Maria didn't stare straight ahead for that would be gazing into the here and the now which is quite a dangerous thing for any person to do. From the corner of her eye, though, she saw a globe of light that had filth contained within it...a light that was moving and tinged with yellow and decay; figures of men were huddled within it and walking toward the house.

Maria slammed the door shut. I stared into my beautiful sister's dark eyes. We embraced.

-You're soaked through and shivering. Come and use the bathroom and get out of those wet things before you catch your death.

For no reason, we laughed and ran side by side up the flight of stairs.

-Did you lock the door?

-No. I kept it open so that thieves may rob us. Of course, I locked it. Why do you ask such a question?

-I don't know. I just wondered. I thought that I was being followed just now.

-Is that why you were screaming? Foolish girl. I already have some coffee brewing. I'll bring it up to you while you change. Here's the guest room.

I took off my trench coat and slipped out of my clothes. I dried my hair but I didn't place a towel around it for I hated doing that. And, there I stood naked in front of the full length mirror. Not so bad...a slim figure with a thin waist and only a few soft spots. I didn't linger over this image.

I put on my sister's white, terry cloth robe and applied the life giving lipstick. Now, I was ready for in a previous life and in an ancient land, I took great care of my appearance. A previous life...what good was it when it brought you into this one?

My sister entered the room.

-And, what is my sister looking so intense for? You want to tell me or, perhaps, I should guess? I have things to tell you.

She put down the tray and brought me over a hot cup of coffee.

-Thank you.

I fumbled in my bag for a cigarette and matches.

-Ramsay, why do you keep smoking? You look very beautiful, but you're getting to be a little too thin. It's nice on the face, though. You should have been a model.

I lit my cigarette and tossed the matches back into my favorite bag.

-It's still raining outside. Thank you for those compliments. And, I like the taste of tobacco.

-I wasn't just complimenting you. I was also scolding you. Your life could have been so much better.

-Is it over? Well, maybe it's close to being over, at any rate.

-Why do you say such a thing? You're still young-

-Liar.

-You should get married, again. Why don't you? You've waited long enough.

-No one, dear sister, could ever accuse you of warming up to a subject. I still love Jeffrey. I thought you understood that.

-I didn't like him, you know.

-I know; but, most people didn't like him. Jeffrey was very austere. Aunt Francesca liked him, though.

-Our parents didn't like him. I feel terrible saying this to you with the way he died... murdered so horribly.

-It's so strange your mentioning Jeffrey tonight because it's the first time I've thought about him all day. I always think about him, you know. Always. But, today, it was different.

I leaned my head back against the headboard and saw my past.

CHAPTER II
DR. BAST

IT WAS the lightning storm that brought it all back to me. It was a kind of visualization of the first time I'd met Jeffrey. I was twenty years old at the time and having dinner with my Aunt Francesca. I had always liked her demeanor and her attitude toward life. She was an attractive and knowledgeable woman who knew how to be discreet.

-Now, let's have a real girl-to-girl talk, Ramsay. What are your plans for this evening? Tell me.

-I thought I'd spend the evening with you, if you don't mind my company too much.

-Of course not, darling, but here put some of my lipstick on. You are such a beautiful young girl and I want you to enhance that beauty.

I remember smiling at her enunciation of every syllable. I took the tube of lipstick from her and applied it.

-Much better. The hair is a little too long and it could be combed out more, but...

I helped myself to another biscuit and applied a generous amount of butter to it. I don't dare do this now!

-Let me tell you of an interesting experience I had the other day. I was attending a lecture at the Theosophical Society boring, really, but it had its moments. A beautiful man sat down next to me. I tried not to stare, but I really could not help myself. His look and manner were so unique. His aura was like that of a deity from another world and, yet, he was so discreet. You are smiling. Do you laugh at your aunt?

-What was his name? He had one, didn't he?

-Jeffrey Bast.

-What kind of a surname is that?

-Egyptian, I think. He asked to meet you.

-Me? You told him about me? Does he want to meet me tonight, in this rain?

-Yes. I will drive you to his office in the city.

-When?

-Now, my dear. I did not tell him about you, Ramsay. He knew that you existed. He saw it and told me. You will have an interesting life with this man.

-I beg your pardon? What exactly are you hinting at?

-Let us get ready to leave.

-Not yet. Tell me more about him, first. Tell me everything you know. I want to hear more of your impressions.

-He is Egyptian, but there is a blend of the Aryan in his blood, as well. He is slim and tall with dark hair and almond shaped eyes that are penetrating...eyes that see.

-See what?

-All that should be perceived by an Adept.

-An Adept? What's that?

My aunt was getting impatient.

-Go upstairs and get your trench coat and put your black heels on. The black dress that you have on now is suitable.

I remember walking upstairs to get ready and stopping in front of the bathroom mirror for a moment to comb my hair and pin it back into place. I slipped into my black heels, pulled my trench coat on and ran downstairs. A car's horn beeped. My aunt wasn't wasting any time.

I ran the short distance from the house to the car and didn't get terribly wet.

-You will catch your death of cold.

-No. I won't. I never get ill. Now, tell me where Mr. Bast lives.

-Dr. Bast.

-Oh? Where does *Dr.* Bast live?

-In Manhattan.

-He must be successful. Is he?

-Yes.

Aunt Francesca started the car and pulled out of her parking spot. I remember staring at her as we drove over the bridge and into the Upper East Side of Manhattan. It was a part of town that I'd never been in. I was a

working girl of middle-class parents and it never occurred to me to open closed doors. However, it would
occur to my Aunt Francesca.

-I will loan you my umbrella, dear. He is waiting inside for you.

-You're not going in with me? I won't go in, then.

-Enter the temple unaided. Do not be afraid. I would
never place you in danger. I will wait here until you are
safely inside.

-How will I get home?

-I will come for you. And, yes, I will know when to
come. Put your fears aside.

Her ruby red lips smiled at me as she flipped her
blonde hair back; a gesture which annoyed my mother
to no end.

I opened the car's door and ran toward the stone
stoop that led to Dr. Bast's office. Was I tempted to look
back in regret for a life left behind? Perhaps. To this day,
I don't know the answer.

I pressed the doorbell. A woman answered and ush-
ered me inside. She must have been on the point of leaving and I think that she resented my calling at so late an
hour. She told me to wait. Now, I was alone in a dark
room. I stood motionless at its center. Slowly, I took off
my trench coat and hung it up on the coat rack. At least,
my hands weren't trembling.

My composure was coming back.

-Miss Cruz?

-Yes!

I turned around, startled. I hadn't heard him come up behind me.

-Forgive me for startling you. I've been told that I walk like a cat and, to an extent, I've the appearance of one. Look...Osiris comes to greet you.

A white, Sphinx cat walked in front of me and sat down.

-He likes you, Miss Cruz. Look at how he stares at you and the intent in his eyes. Come into my office and we'll be more comfortable.

I followed him and the cat followed us. I sat down in the chair opposite his desk never taking my eyes off him. Osiris sat in my lap.

-As you must know, I met your aunt the other day at a meeting of the Theosophical Society; an interesting group of people but rather inert, I'm afraid. They do a great deal of talking but take very little action toward fulfillment. I do. I am a Magus. Do you know what that term means, Ramsay?

-No. Should I?

-You will. I am independent in my studies and, yet, I answer to others. My quest began many years ago when I was chosen to become a member of a Brotherhood. It was the most glorious day of my life and I revel in it still. But, with fortune, comes balance and now I must balance the scales. Do you smoke, Ramsay? Here? Try one of mine. They're a special Turkish blend which are quite strong and delicious.

-Dr. Bast-

-You must call me Jeffrey; for as you know, we are soon to be married.

-Am I to balance things out for you?

-I need to take a wife and your name was mentioned to me by your Aunt Francesca.

He had avoided my question.

-I'll bet. So, she did mention me to you.

-Don't be angry with Francesca, for she thinks highly of you and has only your best interests at heart. Your aunt is a selfish woman, but she does think of you, Ramsay. Her selfishness is a virtue.

-Why do you want to marry me?

-Will you marry me? I implore you to say yes. I beg it of you, if only to satisfy me as a man.

Again, he had avoided my question.

-You haven't answered my questions. But, when we're married, you can answer all my questions. I have many. You can now take me in your arms, if you like.

-I shall, if you'll but allow me to.

-I said that I would.

Jeffrey got up from his chair and came around to my side of the desk. He took my hand and seemed to lift me off the chair. With his right hand, he placed his thumb to the center of my forehead and applied pressure. I felt my body divide itself from within. For a moment, my astral body was "flung" out and rose toward the ceiling. Just as quickly, I re-entered my body and held on to Jeffrey.

Why had I agreed to marry him? Had my aunt's insanity rubbed off on me?

-Are you all right, Ramsay?

-Yes. No. What happened just now? What did you do to me?

-I baptized you. My brotherhood needs us.

-For what?

-I may not tell you that. However, I will tell you that one day I will pass from your life. A period of mourning will follow for several years and, then, you will again regain your footing, if you would, and know what to do.

-I didn't understand any of that, darling, but I don't care. Tomorrow night we'll be married?

-Everything has been arranged.

-What's going to happen?

-You will be spared the procession of death. Others may attempt to stop it.

He kissed me and it was wonderful...wonderful because his breath was sweet and delicious. It was also painful as my breath was taken from my body as he gave me his. He pressed hard against me so that I could feel his manhood.

-Are you very tired?

-I'm wide awake now.

-Good. Your aunt will be here shortly and she will drive us to my home. It's only a short distance uptown.

My Aunt Francesca and Jeffrey had spoken at great length on the previous day. They had made significant plans.

-I hear your aunt calling to us. Come, my dear, we mustn't keep her waiting.

Before I knew it, we were in my Aunt Francesca's car. Jeffrey didn't direct her to his place because she obviously knew where it was. They'd only met yesterday?

CHAPTER III
THE GROUP

MY AUNT Francesca parked her car in front of Jeffrey's brownstone. There were lights on inside and I could see the movement of a shadow cross in front of a Venetian blind on the second floor.

-Do you hesitate, my dear?

It was comfortable in the car and safe...the safety of ignorance or the mindless stupidity of it? Was I about to eat the apple and know of life and death?

-Yes. But, let's go in.

Aunt Francesca followed us in and I could feel her own hesitation and excitement as she touched my back. What had she and Jeffrey discussed at their "first" meeting yesterday?

Jeffrey's house was a manly and sedate place of dark and quiet charm. We took off our coats and walked into the dining room. Jeffrey introduced us to his friends who were soon to become my friends. Some of them, I liked immediately and some I did not. I've always been self-conscience about meeting people for the first time. Jeffrey started the introductions beginning on the right hand side of the table.

Lisa Dunkirk was a small and slender woman in her late twenties and was dressed in black. She was the sort of woman who I would have never chosen as a friend. She was a snob who didn't care about anyone outside of her own sphere. I found her affectations annoying and her sly smile inappropriate. But, she was clever.

-Hello, darling, so pleased to meet you. I'm quite sure we'll be friends, one day. It'll be fun, really.

Lisa was from "old" money and, to hear her talk, quite a large amount of it. However, to hear Aunt Francesca tell of it, it was a sufficient amount to live on and not work. Certain luxury items, more than Lisa would care to admit to, were unattainable to her.

Instead of introducing the woman sitting next to Lisa, Jeffrey introduced the man sitting opposite her. Aunt Francesca noticed this too and we also noticed that no one was sitting at the head of the table or at the opposite end. Jeffrey introduced a tall and thin gentleman in his middle sixties who had the most beautifully chiseled features I'd ever seen. His name was Timothy Fields.

-Good evening, Ramsay.

He nodded to my Aunt Francesca as if they'd already met. I looked at my aunt through the corner of my eye and she turned her own gaze downward.

Timothy was the type of British gentleman I loved to read about in novels and watch on the movie screen. He was a collector of antiques and had access to all the warehouses of every museum in the world; an advantage that both his name and money conferred upon him. His actual collection, though, was not that immense; it contained a select few objects which Timothy used and did not waste on exhibit in a glass case.

A thunder clap was heard, but no one seemed to notice or to care. The fire blazed away and the room felt warm enough. It was then that I noticed the room was in total darkness save for the two candles lit on either side of the long, oak table.

We were next introduced to the woman sitting next to Lisa Dunkirk: Allyson Hendricks. Immediately, I loved this woman as I would my own sister. She was a classic beauty in every sense of that expression. Allyson's jet-black hair was pulled back into a French bun adorned with a white, lace ribbon. She was wearing a black, silk dress with white edgings and on her right hand was a diamond bracelet. Her high cheekbones and lovely blue eyes were mesmerizing.

-Hello, Ramsay.

Allyson smiled and extended her hand to me. She had retired from figure skating. She had had to conquer fears that were not of the trivial kind. She'd had a fear of people and a fear of her own talents as a skater which stayed with her for so many of the crucial years of her career.

Jeffrey introduced us to the man who was sitting next to Timothy Fields: Kenjiro Kaziyama. He was tall and slender and although severe looking, he smiled with his eyes and uttered no word of greeting. He reminded me of Jeffrey.

The woman sitting next to Allyson was Tana. She was a Russian woman who wore too much powder on her face. And, like everyone else, Tana was dressed in black. She lit a cigarette and nodded.

-Ramsay?

The man sitting next to Kenjiro was Armando Castaneda. He wore a black silk suit with a matching black shirt but no tie. He waved his hand in a slight downward motion in greeting. He did not smile. Tall and lean, his long black hair was pulled into a braided ponytail...a look that I'm not all that fond of.

My Aunt Francesca slipped past me and sat in the chair opposite Armando. There was one more person to be introduced: the man sitting next to Armando, a man whose face was covered in bandages.

-Ramsay, this is Mark. He can neither see clearly nor speak at the moment; inconveniences that will most certainly pass with time. Touch his hand, darling, so that he may greet you in his own fashion.

I touched his hand, but he didn't make the slightest response.

-Good. The introductions are at an end. Ramsay, sit here, please, at this end with Mark and Tana to flank you, so to speak. I will sit opposite you at the other end of the table.

He walked to the opposite end of the table and sat down.

-And, now the dinner may commence.

His voice was harsh as he ordered the food to be served by his two servants. The main course was delicious meat cut very fine, almost with surgical precision. The wine was poured and the conversations began.

-Ramsay?

-Yes? I'm sorry. I didn't hear you, Tana.

-Eat your dinner, it's quite delicious, and sample the wine. Jeffrey does spoil us so, but he has always been a generous host and benefactor. You met him through your Aunt Francesca, is that not right or am I mistaken?

-You're right. I've known him for probably the better part of an hour.

-It's not so usual, is it? Are you afraid?

-No. I guess not.

-You had difficulty answering that. You meant to say more. Have some wine.

-I feel an anticipation building up inside of me. It's as if...really, I can't describe it.

That anticipation has grown with the years.

-Yes! I know exactly what you mean, Ramsay. When I was a figure skater, I experienced it at every competition. It's the feeling that builds up inside of you when you're waiting for your turn to perform. Sometimes, it's dread and sometimes it's anxiety; but, always, it's the anticipation of the event. When I begin the program, will I conquer my fear and allow the demiurge to take over or will I be defeated by the fear and the ice? But, usually, my nerves did get the best of me.

Allyson had a light laugh, but I could hear the sadness in her voice. What disappointments had she endured?

-Tell me, Ramsay, about your dreams. Do you remember them or do you not bother? Many people discard their dreams, and that is a pity for they tell us so much.

-I don't remember them, Tana. Does it matter?

-Yes. Yes, it does. It is through our dreams, particularly "epic" dreams, that I came to meet your future husband.

-Jeffrey spoke of others...his superiors.

-We, here, are not of them. I can quite assure you of that. In no way are we the superiors of Jeffrey.

-Then, who are these superiors, Tana? Do you know?

-Drink your wine, dear, and ask no more about them. Your dreams may provide a clue. Remember what I tell you.

Mark sat motionless with his hands folded on the table in front of him. I remember smiling at him and he staring at me through the slits of his bandaged face. As the storm continued to rage, I was able to hear other conversations at the table.

-Jeffrey, sweet, I like the dear girl and it does bring us just a bit closer to-

-Lisa, don't speak of it. You don't know everything and you'd only be making educated guesses.

-So true. But, one is almost anxious to get on with it. It's the waiting that drives one quite mad.

-Enjoy this waiting period while you're able to, Lisa. You should revel in the familiar for soon it will be lost to us forever.

-I wish you wouldn't put it quite like that. You can be brutal.

-I know of no other way to phrase it.

-Allyson?

-Yes, Armando?

-What do you do to fill up your time now that you're no longer a figure skater? Life must be boring for you.

-No, Armando, it's not boring at all. I still skate for my own satisfaction.

-Is it safe at your age?

-Yes, Armando, it's quite safe and a lot of fun, too. I don't have to worry about being scored.

-But, one must have fun, Armando, for it rounds off the character and the personality. We'll need our sense of fun, eh, Jeffrey?

Jeffrey didn't answer Timothy. Instead, he stared down the length of the table at me and, then, he directed his stare at Mark.

-Francesca, tell us of the dream that you had the other night, if you want to. If not, please forgive my asking.

-How odd that you should ask about that, Kenjiro. At first, I thought that I was observing myself on the astral level...the ethereal plane, you know.

-Yes, darling, we know.

-Of course, Lisa. But, for that to have been true, I would have had to create the surroundings that I found myself in. I did not do that for I did not have the desire to do it. I found myself walking down the street of my childhood neighborhood which was congested with buildings. There was a group of young people gathering on one of the stoops. They noticed me and started to taunt me in an underhanded manner; but, this did not concern me at all. As I approached the stoop, a clear, grey film immersed everything...it was quite sinister.

Aunt Francesca paused for a moment to sip her wine.

-I entered the building and walked into the first floor apartment. The rooms were just as I remembered them, but everything seemed so fragile that at the slightest touch of a finger it would disintegrate to powder. I heard voices upstairs and found myself in that apartment with my sister, Anais, who is Ramsay's mother. There were others there, as well, but I did not recognize them.

Aunt Francesca was close to tears as she struggled to continue with her story.

-My sister and I left the apartment and walked upstairs to another apartment which was filthy! A chain from the ceiling came down and struck me. The dream ended. This world that I had entered seemed abandoned and dead with only a few people left within it. A great agonizing pity ran through my heart for my sister. She was alone and I was visiting her out of kindness. Jeffrey, I feel that this dream was a prophecy.

-It signaled the end of the world, Francesca.

-My God! How you say that with such finality!

A silence descended upon the room that one could actually touch. I wanted to scream and run, but I felt paralyzed.

Lisa broke that silence. We were all grateful.

-Jeffrey, darling, I'd love to share my dream. I've been thinking about nothing else all day and I quite need to get it off my chest.

-Dreams shouldn't disturb you.

-This one did, dear Jeffrey. It was so real and I watched myself die in it. Ghastly.

-And, you lived to tell of it?

-Yes, Armando, darling, I live to tell of it. Must you always be so cynical? May I speak Jeffrey?

-Please, Lisa.

-I was with a group of people...people who I knew in the dream, but not people I know in this life. We were in a stone chamber of some sort...trapped in some prison. On the other side of the wall was a vampire reaching through the bars to get at us. The bars and the stones that encased him were giving way most dreadfully...the creaking and the powder from the stones. We were trying to carve a piece of wood into a stake, but it was taking too long.

Lisa paused for effect.

-The stones gave way and everything came crashing in as some of us tried to make a run for it. It was then that a young girl got the unfinished stake and drove it through the monster's heart. I didn't actually see this, but I knew it. We stopped running and went back in to have a look around, but there was no body to be seen anywhere...only some dried parchment with writing on it which I scooped up.

Lisa stopped to ponder her own words.

-Curious, you know...anyway, it disintegrated in my hands before I could read a word of it. And, then, a hand...reached for my throat and began choking the life out of me. It was the vampire! I could actually feel the enjoyment he was having...the sweet and vengeful hatred...such purity of hate. I stepped out of my body to watch the deed. It finished and left me for dead.

-What did this vampire look like?

-Tall and white...the face was like paste. And, it was broad daylight when he killed me, Jeffrey. He was covered from head to foot in a black robe.

The clock chimed the hour of midnight. We sat there and listened with the comforting darkness of night surrounding us.

-The specter of death cannot be defeated, but an escape may be possible, Lisa. Good. It's stopped raining outside, and I'm certain that if you look out the window to the east, you'll see a full moon at its zenith. Let us repair to the drawing room.

Jeffrey handed out the brandy and the cigarettes. I stayed close to my Aunt Francesca. I wasn't tired, but I felt that I wanted to go home; not knowing then that I would never go home. I sipped the brandy and smoked one of Jeffrey's Turkish cigarettes. I have them especially made to this day. I can afford to do these things because my husband left me a wealthy woman.

Aunt Francesca spoke to me as Tana stood there and listened. Lisa and Allyson were speaking to Jeffrey and Armando while Timothy and Kenjiro were discussing something quite heatedly. Mark sat on a chair with his hands in his lap and said nothing.

-Ramsay? Ramsay?

-Yes? I'm listening, Aunt Francesca.

-But, you keep staring at Mark. You should not. It is Jeffrey whom you will marry soon. Look at him and follow his movements. Learn the art of being a host from him.

-Yes.

-Then, do it.

-How long have you known these people?

-Ramsay, Tana is standing here. It is impolite to ask that question.

-I don't mind, Francesca. The girl has a right to know. She has a right to know everything. However, it is Jeffrey who must tell her these things. But, ladies, let me tell you of my dream. The darkness and the candles augment my tale very well for it is much more than a dream.

I glanced at the candles as Tana continued to speak.

-I call it an epic dream. It has no beginning and no end for those terms are meaningless. I had entered another universe. I was within a huge craft that floated through space. The craft seemed to dwarf the very space that contained it. I floated through this spaceship and my physical form kept varying. I drifted in a direct line and-

Jeffrey continued Tana's story as if he'd had the dream, himself.

-Ladies, we must begin with an analogy. When one places a phonograph record upon the spinning disc and, then, places the diamond upon said disc, vibration is emitted...a sound, if you will. If one flips the disc over on its reverse side and, again, places the diamond point upon it, more vibration is heard, but of a different quality and degree.

-Yes! Vibration, Jeffrey. That's what kept emanating from everywhere and from all that I touched...a sound...a celestial sound that was almost...holy. It was as if God stood at the threshold of this spacecraft.

-You slipped into the edge of another universe and another time, Tana. For a moment, you were locked into the "groove" of the disc. Your form kept changing because you lacked the skill to master the situation. It was your soul which made the journey and not your astral body.

-Jeffrey, what is the significance of my dream?

He looked at Tana with the keenness of a hunter's eyes.

-You know its significance. You have given clues to your own nature and to an unsolved puzzle; although, of course, that was not your intention. Thank you.

-Did that also happen to Lisa and Aunt Francesca?

-No, Ramsay. Jeffrey left us standing there in the dark room while he made his way to the three arguing gentlemen. My aunt laughed.

-He is working the room as a good host should; and, as you, my dear, should also do.

-Why?

-Tana, would you excuse us, please, for I must take my niece aside and speak to her in private.

-Of course, Francesca. I see that Allyson is alone, so I'll talk with her.

My aunt lit another cigarette and so did I. Was I already beginning to smoke too much?

-Ramsay, listen to me, please.

-I am.

-You have duties now to Jeffrey and to all of your guests here tonight. You must mingle among them and speak to them and come to know them as your own friends. In time, they will be your friends.

-What is this all about?

-I knew you would ask that question. I love you so! Ask it of Jeffrey and not of me. I am only beginning to learn of things and events to come.

-Will Jeffrey and I be married here tonight- this morning? It really is early morning now, isn`t it?

-Yes. Now, let us speak to the others.

The four men were having a discussion regarding the concept of time. Mark was not among them. He sat upright in his chair and continued to stare straight ahead. Aunt Francesca placed herself between me and his line of vision.

-There! Now, he can stare at me if he wants to. I have had enough of his gazing and do not turn around, young lady.

Allyson must have overheard us. She went over to Mark and spoke to him. Why hadn't I gone over to him and spoken to him?

Tana and Lisa approached the men. Kenjiro was speaking.

-How can one designate a meaning for the term time? It has no meaning; merely a man-made definition of the function as we perceive its function. Time is composed of motion and light which are two inseparable phenomena. Time is measured and not defined: it is measured by the components of light and their relationship to bodily movement.

-Celestial movement, Kenjiro.

-Jeffrey, please continue. I find Kenjiro's explanation confusing, somewhat.

Armando smiled at Jeffrey with respect and longing. My Aunt Francesca noticed this and glanced at his crotch. Of course, Armando being a vain man, thrilled at the glance although it did not arouse him. Kenjiro continued.

-Celestial movement is contained within the shell of the universe, the casing or the shield, if you like, that protects and entraps us.

-Perhaps, barrier would be a better term, Kenjiro?

-Yes, Timothy...a barrier...the sphere that binds it all together...the light and the motion and the many anomalies.

-Protects us and shields us from what? Are we in danger?

Armando laughed at my question. I wanted to slap him. I would have, too, if he hadn't been Jeffrey's friend.

-Yes, Ramsay. We're in danger from seeing and knowing too much.

-Seeing God?

Kenjiro was patient with me.

-From seeing the purity of all that is Holy, Ramsay; that is the way I will put it to you. It is the way that you can comprehend it now. In time, you will dismiss my explanation. In my dream experience there was no time. I wasn't held down by consciousness dominated by a physical entity. Perhaps, a separation from this world would free us from the bonds of time? Are we not carried along by the rotation of the sphere?

Timothy made his request between puffs on his cigarette.

-I overheard the conversation about your dream, Tana. Jeffrey, please give us your view on this. I heard the analogy, but I want your opinions and, of course, your beliefs.

I looked out the window and into the darkness which was feebly lit by a street light. The room inside was filled with smoke and the haze from our cigarettes could be seen in halos around the flames of the candles.

-Tana's soul, Timothy, was taken from her body and placed within another universe. It was a universe that is still in its primitive stages of creation. Tana's soul, although not physical, is composed of substance and, therefore, it has adaptive properties.

-Do you mean it has an instinct to survive?

-No, Tana. It has the quality of thought and to assimilate itself within its adapted container.

-Fascinating. Jeffrey, you raise many question in my mind; and, I will put forth each one of them. Forgive my curious mind, but I feel that we must know all that can be learned from Tana's experience the other night.

-You're quite right, Kenjiro. Please ask me anything you like.

-You tell us that her soul was taken from her body and, yet, she stands here before us tonight. How is this possible? When the body gives up the ghost, it no longer lives.

-By ghost, you do mean to say-

-Do not interrupt me, Armando. You know what I mean. Your feigned ignorance doesn't amuse me. I think you a fool! When the body releases the celestial breath it dies.

-You are correct, friend, but the soul was taken and Tana did not give it up.

-Taken by whom and for what purpose, Jeffrey?

-I will explain, Kenjiro, and all of you listen. Mark, you must listen, as well. Get yourself a brandy and join us.

Jeffrey's voice had become hard but not cruel. We all watched Mark slowly get up and make his way to the small bar. He seemed to be in pain and my heart ached for him. I made to go to him, but my Aunt Francesca held me back. Allyson went to him, instead, and poured him a brandy.

-Good. Sip it.

Mark put the brandy glass to his bandaged face and sipped at the liquid. Allyson watched him with love and pain in her eyes.

Jeffrey continued.

-Had Tana awakened, her body would have had movement and even intelligence, but there would have been no emotion or wisdom and, perhaps, a physical immortality would have resulted. Yes... Kenjiro, I've not answered your question just yet, but I am about to.

We waited and I could feel the pressure from the physical confines of the room; every portion of the room seemed to emit a sound. Hadn't Tana spoken of sound and pressure?

-Tana's soul was taken by one of the ancient architects of our universe. He took the soul to test its timbre, if you would. You should be pleased, Tana.

-An ancient architect, you say? A god?

-Yes. An entity whom we would consider a god.

Kenjiro thanked Jeffrey for his answers and retired to the sofa.

Mark dropped his brandy glass and bent down to retrieve it. Fortunately, it had been drained and the glass wasn't broken. He had difficulty in bending so Allyson scooped it up for him and placed it on an end table.

CHAPTER IV
THE WEDDING

THE GROUP dispersed except for Allyson, Mark, and me.

-It's been a long evening. I'm so tired and there's still so much left to do.

-What's left to do? Have we even started?

Allyson was surprised at my statement, but recovered and took my hand.

-Why don't we go upstairs where we can speak in private, Ramsay? Mark, will you come with us? We shouldn't walk through the hallways alone; it may not be safe.

-Not safe? I don't like the way you said that. What are we not safe from? Intruders? Please tell me.

-Later. Mark, would you come with us, please?

Mark nodded and the three of us made ready to leave the drawing room. We walked through the dark hallway with Allyson leading the way and me and Mark following. She held the candle to light the way through what seemed like pitch blackness. How could the inside of a house be so unnaturally dark?

We reached the main staircase and ascended it. At the top of the stairs, I could see the eyes of a cat reflecting the light of Allyson's candle: it was Osiris waiting for us. As I passed by the cat, I stooped down to pick him up and hold him in my arms. He was very light and affectionate and, to this day, he lives.

Allyson stopped in front of a door, reached into her pocket and extracted a key. She opened the door and felt on the wall for the light switch.

-It's not working. It's all right, though, we'll be fine. Mark, would you have a look around inside first? Thank you.

Mark edged by us and walked into the dark room with no candle and no light to see by. We waited.

-What's taking him so long? Is the room so big and dark?

-He'll be out soon. Mark is thorough and precise. I hear his footsteps now.

He walked out of the room and edged by us.

-Let's go in, Ramsay. Mark will stand guard outside the door.

I held my tongue and followed her into a dark bedroom. Allyson walked over to the mirror which was set against the wall and placed the candle on the floor.

-Ramsay would you close the door, please. Thank you.

-Will Mark be all right outside in the hallway like that?

-Do you worry about him?

-I do.

-Why?

-I feel like I've known him for such a long time.

-Does it matter?

-Will he be all right?

-Yes. He's guarding the door against trespassers. Look over at the bed, Ramsay, your wedding gown is ready.

Allyson walked over to a bed that I could barely see and lifted the white sequined gown. It sparkled like the stars of the night had they been placed on a white silk canvas. The line of the gown came straight down and the waist was encrusted with a diamond belt. Allyson held the gown before her.

-I hope you like it. I designed it myself and I did much of the embroidery and detail work, too. I didn't dare trust it to anyone else. You do like it? I used to design my skating outfits based on ideas I got from magazines.

-I love it! But, please, tell me what's going on. Who are you...who is everyone else? What is this all about?

-Hasn't Jeffrey told you anything? He must have said something.

-Not enough.

Allyson brought the gown over and held it out for me to take. I took it and caressed it.

-I can tell you this much: from tonight on, your life will no longer be safe. You and your Aunt Francesca were the final pieces of our puzzle and now the portrait is complete; but there are murderers who want to steal and destroy the portrait.

I didn't ask any more questions of Allyson. She seemed distraught about my curiosity and I sensed her concern that she had, perhaps, revealed too much to me.

Someone knocked on the door.

-That will be Mark. We must hurry.

Allyson pinned my hair back and smoothed out any ruffled spots on the gown. She asked me a simple question.

-Are you ready?

-I think so. I don't know. Can't my Aunt Francesca come up? I want to see her.

-That's not possible right now. You'll see her later. Now, look at yourself in the mirror. Go ahead.

I did as Allyson said, but I could barely see my image. My eyes weren't adjusting to the darkness; there wasn't enough candle light in the room.

-Why can't there be more candles or an oil lamp or something? This is maddening! I hate it!

-Ramsay, calm down. We have to go into the main chamber now. Please...do your best to control your emotions. Don't be like me, always a nervous wreck before anything.

We laughed, but the hysteria growing within me only turned inward, not quite releasing itself. Allyson adjusted her own dress; and, for a moment, her hand reached up to pat her neatly folded hair it its new white laced bun.

-Let's go.

Allyson picked up the candle and we made to leave the room. I followed her out, but just before I crossed the threshold, I turned back. The darkness was giving way to light and a ray of the sun spanned the floor of the room.

Allyson took my hand and pulled me away while Mark closed the door behind us. Carefully, we made our way up a spiral staircase and, then, down a long and narrow corridor. Mark followed us and I had such a wild urge to break loose from Allyson's hold and run into his arms...and just run away with him. I wanted to do that. I would have done that... but my curiosity...it had to be satisfied.

We stopped in front of what appeared to be utter blackness.

Was I marrying out of curiosity?

Yes.

Was I marrying for a privileged lifestyle?

Yes.

Was I marrying out of love?

No.

Then, why? In God's name, why?

Was it such a blind and complete trust that I had in my aunt or was it simply the old- fashioned tradition of being married by barter?

The utter blackness opened and revealed a point of light from within. The three of us stepped forward into the chasm of pointed lights as the door gently closed behind us. Allyson let go of my hand and someone else took it. It was Jeffrey. He was dressed in a black, silk kaftan that reached to the floor. His feet were bare and he wore no article of jewelry.

We moved, or at least I assumed that we did, for I sensed no direction or compass point in this...room? Had I the courage to look up, I would have seen stars in the night sky.

We stopped and I could make out the dim outline of what appeared to be an altar. It was long and rectangular and a few objects had been placed upon it. Jeffrey left me for a moment and went to the altar. He came back and handed me a gold chalice which I assumed was filled with wine. I was mistaken.

-Drink my blood.

I did. And, then, we approached the altar and knelt down before it. A bright disc of solar light appeared overhead. Its light and heat grew in intensity although its circumference remained constant. The sun, for that's what it was, illuminated the room as the other sun would illuminate the planet during the noon hour.

At last, I saw where we were: in a different and ancient time in the land of the Eternal Sun and the ancient gods. Beneath my feet was the sand of the desert and the celestial markers: the pyramids.

We moved toward one of these pyramids. Jeffrey held my hand and the other eight people present followed us as we walked directly into the very side of the structure.

Jeffrey spoke.

-Our ancestors, my dear Ramsay, needed no door-ways.

The ten of us walked through a stone passage which had many sharp turns in it. We had no difficulty in making our way because the light from the sun flooded into the pyramid and lit our way as it penetrated the very pores of the stone. I could feel us ascending the pyramid. Jeffrey never once looked at me as he kept his gaze straight ahead.

We reached the top chamber and our processional came to a halt. As if on cue, everyone took up their designated places: Lisa and Timothy stood in the northern quadrant, Allyson and Mark stood in the east, Aunt Francesca and Kenjiro stood toward the western wall, and Tana and Armando stood in the southern quadrant. Jeffrey and I stood in the center of the chamber.

We waited until the sun began its descent. Jeffrey put his arm about me.

-Remember the light, dearest Ramsay. It is precious and neither one of us will see its brilliance again for a very long time. Save me, dear Ramsay.

-Save you from what, Jeffrey?

-From myself and from my enemies. No more words must be spoken. The witnesses here will remember and record this...this our marriage ceremony.

I remember closing my eyes and still the solar flame penetrated even that darkness. I could feel Jeffrey's hand caressing my breasts and then gliding down to that soft spot. Did I faint at that moment? Did time collapse in upon itself? I don't remember. Or, had I imagined it all? Had it been an event enacted in my mind?

-Ramsay? Ramsay?

-What is it? What do you want? How did I come to wear this?

-I helped you on with it. I'll leave now through the other door.

-Allyson?

-I must leave. I can't stay.

-What do I do now? Tell me, please.

-Go to him.

Allyson opened the door and left. I turned away to look in the mirror. I was wearing a white negligee. I looked around the small room as the lights faded to a soft rose color.

I opened the door and walked into the other room: a bedroom which was spacious and dark. I walked toward the large bed set in the center of the room. What I saw brought a smile to my face and, perhaps, even a little fear to the heart; but that was good because fear is needed in love and sex.

Jeffrey was lying naked on the bed. I walked closer to him until my body touched the sheets. His body was beautiful; slim and tight with no body hair at all except in that one place where my eyes were transfixed. He touched himself...he caressed it with his hand.

-Disrobe and make love to it. I want to feel your beautiful lips, dearest Ramsay, on the crown of my manhood. Disrobe!

I did as he ordered me to do. The authority of his cultured and demanding voice excited me. Yes. This is as it should be. In one swift gesture, I took off the clinging negligee and climbed softly on to the bed to obey my husband.

-Kneel down before me and do as I've told you.

I touched the hard tower lightly and lovingly as my fingers encircled the thick shaft. I lowered my head to its head, parted my lips and drew out my tongue to taste the clear fluid which formed a tiny pool on the opening. I tasted it. Exquisite!

Jeffrey's hand stroked the nape of my neck...he mussed my hair...as I bent down to taste his flesh and sperm. Greedily, I kissed the tip and quickly took his manhood into my mouth.

-Good.

I withdrew and kissed the hard shaft and, again, I placed it back into my mouth. I went down further and took more of the alabaster weapon...and more still...working my tongue along the deliciously hard tower. I began to choke, but I didn't care if I should drop dead choking; it was my wedding present and I wanted all of it. With his hand, Jeffrey pushed my head further down until my mouth almost touched his soft, dark pubic hair.

His hand moved between my legs and he clutched at my moist spot. It hurt terribly, but it felt wonderful! He could have ripped me apart and my pleasure wouldn't have been lessened. But, I had to come up for air...slowly...I rested my face against the magical weapon. Jeffrey flung me down on to the mattress and lay on top of me.

-Ramsay, I'll answer all your questions and, yet, none of them. We must complete our wedding night.

He drew me to him and kissed me long and passionately. I thought his tongue would reach down into my throat. He entered me hard and with no emotion of love or hate for it was a sensual act and passion was the only force necessary to ignite it.

I felt the blood dripping down to the sheets, pouring forth from my open body with Jeffrey's tower embedded in it. Blood was now on that spiritual and most powerful of magical weapons. It excited my husband and his erection grew thicker. He lifted himself up and me with him, holding on to me with his strong hands. I opened my eyes and looked into his dark eyes.

-Look around you, Ramsay. Know where you are and remember all that you see.

I did as he ordered and saw redness fading into the black sky. I saw distant stars and the transparent film of the Milky Way.

-It's beautiful.

-You look at yourself. You are the night sky, goddess of the heavens whose radiance fluctuates within the Unity. The most beautiful of all the illusions. Your blood excites me and my sperm will soon flow into you...the material giving substance and life to that which is untouched. I give life to the darkness of heaven as my fluid plants a seed into the void. My weapon, darling, is your slave as I am your master. You will not join the professional of death. You and the others at my table tonight will leave that unholy line and journey elsewhere.

-What procession of death?

-It will mark the end of all that is known. You may, indeed, be forced to reacquaint yourself with the forgotten arts of your past lives. I tell you this and listen carefully. The ten of us must live. If the illusion of death descends upon any one of us, that illusion must be lifted.

Jeffrey looked deep into my eyes.

-You may find yourself utterly alone one day and, then, you will know what to do. Look into your soul's past and focus upon the mirror that reflects all that ever was.

Jeffrey screamed a deafening blast of air as he reached orgasm. His tower swelled inside of me and I thought it would burst through my body. Gently, he lowered me and lay still on top of me for a long time.

He got up and walked over to the door that I had used to enter the room.

-Get dressed and go into my study. We must leave soon and you must be ready.

He made to leave the room. I got up and threw on the negligee and followed him out.

-Jeffrey, wait! Don't go.

I nearly fell in the darkness. He turned to face me. I stared at his manhood; it still looked so full of life.

-Kiss it once more and, then, we must go.

He forced me to my knees and pulled my head to the thick crown that was still wet and dripping with his life. I kissed it greedily.

-Enough. Now, get to your feet. All your clothes are by the chair over there.

He walked out of the room and I was left to myself. I didn't stop to think of what would occur next or why anything had occurred at all, because to have done so would have been stupid of me; it might have opened the door to regrets.

Clothes had been carefully arranged for me; a woman must have arranged them because all the under-clothes were folded quite properly. I dressed but not without noticing the fine quality of all these garments. Everything felt so comfortable and fitted so beautifully that I almost felt like a different woman. But, wasn't I a different woman?

I looked at my reflection in the full length mirror; the black dress was simple and flattering and deceptively discreet; the short sleeves were slightly draped and so was the hemline...and while not entirely open at the back, there was a small, oval parting in the center exposing my white skin.

I slipped my feet into the black high heels and picked up my new handbag. Naturally, I checked the contents: new cosmetics and a patent leather wallet that was stuffed with money and credit cards and a set of keys to my new home.

I walked down the dark corridor and opened the door to Jeffrey's study. Everyone who had been at the dinner table was present with the exception of Jeffrey. But, I hadn't expected him to be there just yet.

The women approached me and wished me the best. Lisa spoke first.

-Darling, as soon as you're back, we must shop. I'll take you to all the right places. Trust me. Fabulous outfit, by the way. Jeffrey does have *superb* taste.

-Ramsay, our new lives have begun. Tell me that you are happy, my dearest.

-Your aunt is right, Ramsay. You are now embarking on a new life and, perhaps, even another one after this.

-Let her enjoy the present, Tana.

-Why, Allyson? The waiting for Ramsay will soon begin, as well. Perhaps, Jeffrey will soothe her nerves even then, no?

-You've said enough, Tana.

-Perhaps too much for delicate sensibilities? I will stop speaking. I don't want to offend.

The men came to me.

-Jeffrey will tell you how each of us can be reached. I'll always be here for you.

-Thank you, Timothy.

-Ramsay, call me when you and Jeffrey are back in town, will you? The group gets together Fridays for ritual and prayer. Are you aware of that?

-A wise man knows when to be discreet, Armando. Again, your tone betrays you. I must apologize for my friend's-

-Rudeness? I wasn't aware, Kenjiro, that I was being rude in any form. Was I, Ramsay?

-No. Not really.

-Ah, but you're a lady and you wouldn't tell me if I were being rude. I wasn't.

-Enough of this small talk, Armando.

-As you say, Kenjiro. Want to say something else?

Kenjiro wanted to say much more.

-Ramsay, time is now at your disposal, but you must not waste a moment of that precious luxury. Jeffrey has asked me to give you certain necessary instructions and this must not be delayed for any reason.

I noticed that Mark was standing in a corner leaning against the wall. What was he thinking?

My Aunt Francesca led me away from the group of people.

-And, still, you look at that man! The others have noticed; do you know that?

-I'm sorry.

-Simply do not do it anymore. Jeffrey will be here soon and, then, we must all leave.

-Aunt Francesca, what time and what day is it?

-It is Saturday night, but really it is Sunday morning. Why do you ask?

-Just curious. I thought more time had passed.

-You must be disoriented. I understand.

-What is everyone here waiting for? And, don't avoid my question;; you know perfectly well what I mean.

-Then, give me a chance to answer it. When you come back from your honeymoon in Egypt both Jeffrey and Kenjiro will instruct you in the arts of the esoteric. There is much to learn.

-Go on.

-I cannot. I have been told things that even I still cannot comprehend.

-You're afraid, aren't you?

-No.

-Yes. You are, dear aunt. I can see it in your eyes.

She turned away from me and looked at Mark. Even in the darkened room with the drawn curtains, I saw his blue eyes. My aunt turned back to face me.

-All right, then, I admit it. Perhaps, it is my ignorance that keeps me sane for the time being.

-What are you afraid of?

-Must we speak of it?

-Speak of what? Tell me!

-Jeffrey will tell you. Ask me no more, Ramsay.

-I've upset you.

-I've told your family of the marriage. They had to know.

-You did that? Jeffrey and I should have gone to them. Why did you do that Aunt Francesca? Why?

-Lower your voice. It was necessary and your husband gave me leave to do it.

-I didn't give you leave to do it. But, if Jeffrey did...then, it's all right, I suppose.

-Good. I am very glad to hear you speak that way. You speak as a wife should speak.

-Well...how did they take it? I'm almost afraid to ask.

-How do you think? Not well at all. They hate me now, for sure. And, you should thank me for taking the brunt of it for you. They blame me, of course; and I could not argue with them. It was a nasty scene!

-I don't mean to smile, but I can see it all so clearly. I'm surprised you got out alive.

-That is something that you should not joke about anymore. And, what are you smiling about now, dear niece?

-What happened to Mark?

-From what I have gathered, it was a terrible accident during a ritual: an oil lamp exploded and engulfed him in flames.

-How did it happen?

-He was holding the lamp — and there is no need to look past me at him — and there must have been too much oil contained in it. Kenjiro is treating him and Allyson has told me that he will pretty much recover in time, although there will be many tiny scars about the hands and the face from the shards of glass. He's lucky he was not blinded.

-Do Allyson and Mark love each other?

-She loves him and, I believe her affection is returned. Allyson is coming over.

-Jeffrey is here. Francesca, we'll see the newlyweds downstairs to the car and come back up for a nightcap.

I remember stepping out of my body and looking at the closing scene in that room. The men and women gathered around us to wish us well except for Mark.

Jeffrey looked handsome in his dark, pin-stripe suit, but everyone in that room was handsome and beautiful. I thought Allyson the most beautiful...a princess who had come to life and moved among us mortals...so sublime and gracious. I was later to learn that Jeffrey had indeed assumed the part of Pygmalion with her.

Lisa, despite her catty nature, was elegant and well spoken; and, I couldn't help but like her, eventually. She was amusing and knew how to help one forget their troubles for the moment. She taught me the art of conversation and how one can often learn things from people and, yet, offer little information about themselves; a priceless art, that.

All so handsome and beautiful and, yet, each had a darkness that could be felt and not spoken of. It pervaded the room...except for Mark. He was the spark of brightness. Mark did not isolate himself from us, it was we who kept apart from him and the blinding light that his presence symbolized.

CHAPTER V
NIGHTMARE

AS JEFFREY and I stepped outside into the still dark morning, I felt tears welling up in my eyes. I brushed them away and in the process made a complete mess of my face. Jeffrey helped me into the car and, then, got in and slammed the door shut. He signaled the driver to proceed.

-We'll spend a few days in Egypt and, then, return home. Upon our return, you'll spend valuable time with Kenjiro and myself. Do you accept all that? It will be difficult.

-I think my life has a purpose now. Does it?

-I wouldn't have phrased it that way. Your life now has intent. Don't look so perplexed; are you?

-A little.

-It's all right to be confused; it propels you to move forward.

The rest of our journey was made in comparative silence. I thought of my Aunt Francesca and Allyson who were at that moment enjoying a nightcap together. I envied them because I so wanted to be with them. What were they saying? Was I an object of curiosity or ridicule, or had I no place in their thoughts?

The plane ride to Egypt was tedious. The cabin was dark and Jeffrey insisted that the shades be drawn. Few people were on that flight; I know because I looked around and walked the length of the aircraft. The stewardesses were attentive, but I didn't care for their fawning manner. Jeffrey ignored them.

At last, I sat down and slept a strange and dreadful sleep in which I prophesied the deaths of my new friends. All of them were seated on the aisle seats with the men on the left and the women on the right. Mark was standing at the head of the aisle. I walked toward him, but someone grabbed a hold of my arm. It was my Aunt Francesca.

-Ramsay, you must bring me back to life. Don't allow my body to rot. Promise me in front of witnesses, I beg you.

-Darling, I don't want to die, but one must, you know. I suppose it's rather inevitable, really, not that one looks forward to it or at least no one I would care to associate with. Don't let the old ghost hover too long.

-Lisa, what are you saying to me?

-You know why he married you, don't you? Someone should have told you.

-Oh, Armando? Suppose that I do? What business is that of yours? Try answering me for a change.

-You wouldn't like the answer or, perhaps, you wouldn't understand it. I couldn't blame you for that.

-You know what I think?

-Tell me, bitch.

-I see how you look at my husband. I'm not quite as naïve as you think. I do know about these things, but I don't judge you. I've no cause to judge you, yet.

-Forgive me and bring me back.

-I don't like to see a man beg. You're starting to bore me, Armando.

I pulled myself away and ran toward Mark, but I tripped and fell in the darkness. I picked myself up and began to cry.

-Let me help you. Stop struggling like some caged animal.

-Let me go, Timothy!

-I told you to stop your struggling.

-Since when do I listen to you?

-Don't be a little fool! Where are you running to? You're on an airplane and your escape routes are limited, rather.

-No one tells me what to do.

-Indeed? Not even Jeffrey? He'll be interested to know that. I'd like to see his reaction.

-Jeffrey?

-Whom else do you think I mean? Mark? We've all noticed. You haven't been discreet.

In a panic, I pulled away from Timothy. I ran toward Mark, once again; but there was some force dragging me toward the plane's door. I screamed when I saw the door opening. The blast of air struck me like a hammer across the face. Timothy grabbed me.

-Question everything, but keep those questions to yourself. Listen!

-I am! Don't let go of me!

-Whether or not you love Jeffrey is irrelevant to everything; but, the fact that you are his wife is relevant to everything!

-Pardon me for the intrusion. Are you having doubts about me, Ramsay? Don't bother answering; it was a rhetorical question. The regrets and your temporary insanity will ease with time. Let her go, Timothy. The door has been closed.

-As you wish, Jeffrey.

Timothy released me, but the insanity had not stopped.

-Ramsay, bring me back from the dead beautiful and intact.

-I think you're all insane! Bring you back from the dead- how, Tana? You're not talking about reincarnation or vampirism-

-You're beginning to sense the truth.

-No one can come back from the dead, Kenjiro.

-I brought you into Jeffrey's presence. I did that. It took many months of careful planning. Now, you must show your gratitude.

-What are you saying, Aunt Francesca? You lied to me. It was all a pack of lies to trick me into marrying a stranger. I hate you for that. I hate you!

-Ramsay, people have come back from the dead. What of Jesus, Lazarus, and Aeneas? It has been done, my dear wife.

I woke up.

-Ramsay?

-I'm sorry...forgive me, Jeffrey.

-You've had a nightmare

-I'll say!

-An unusual nightmare that frightened you.

-It was...not a prophecy, but a revelation?

-Then, it wasn't a nightmare?

-You know what I dreamt, don't you?

-What is a dream but a creation from thought? Isn't our universe a creation from the purest thought? Yes. I know what you dreamt, Ramsay. We'll say no more about it.

CHAPTER VI
EGYPT

WE LANDED in Cairo just past midnight. As we stepped off the plane, I realized that I had brought no luggage with me. Jeffrey got us through customs with little difficulty. We got into a taxi and headed south, but not to the great pyramid as I thought we would. Instead, we headed toward the ancient city of Memphis. The driver drove at break neck speed and I held tightly on to Jeffrey.

-Does he want to kill us?

-I don't think so, Ramsay.

-There are better ways of doing it.

Clinging to this mysterious man, I looked out the window and found myself staring at desolation. The moon was still high in the night sky and stars draped the velvet cloth of night; but, the beauty above us was not matched by that which surrounded us. We passed by tiny huts and drove straight through small villages which seemed to be composed of dust.

Jeffrey read my thoughts.

-It's unattractive, isn't it? It saddens me that our culture has disintegrated to such a horrific extent. However, we should not despair for far greater glories await.

We were wrapped in a blanket to protect us from the cold of the desert. I should tell you that the year was 1947. Throughout our reckless drive, I had the feeling that a war had just been waged...a war that had ended with the promise of still another one to come and of an enemy that still roamed.

-When ancient Memphis fell, Ramsay, it was the beginning of the end and, yet, that end has been postponed by the surviving Illuminati. The place that we go to now was once the site of an ancient temple. The portion which was once above ground no longer exists except in the phantasmal realm, of course. We'll set foot upon its holy soil and you will see into the temple which is hidden below...intact!

Jeffrey stared with great intent at me.

-Do you know the import of those words, Ramsay? Nothing has been desecrated; all remains as it was and as it should be; all its secrets...all the sacred scrolls and magical weapons untouched by the profane. Look! We approach. Driver, stop the car, at once.

We were jerked forward by the sudden stop. I saw Jeffrey reaching into his jacket. He drew out a gun.

-What are you doing? In the name of God, Jeffrey-don't!

I was powerless to do anything but watch in horror. Jeffrey cocked the pistol and shot the man point blank in the back of the head. I screamed and turned away. I could hear the driver's body slump forward in his seat. I'm still not over it. I was prepared to hate Jeffrey...I wanted to hate him.

-No one must know of our visit here, least of all that dead cretin whom you mourn. The hour grows late.

-I'm not getting out of the car.

-Do you prefer that of a d dead man's company to mine? I should be insulted and angry.

-He was a human being and people may have been waiting for him to come home; people who were depending on him. And, now, they wait for a man who'll never return.

-You're being maudlin. There was no one depending on this man. He was a drug dealer and the lowest of the scum.

-You're laughing at me.

-We're just outside the perimeter of the temple. Take your shoes off or carry them with you, if you like.

I took them off and carried them. They were the only pair of shoes that I had with me. Jeffrey bent over to take off his shoes and socks. He stuffed the socks into his shoes and carried them. He caught me staring at him.

-They're the only pair of shoes I brought.

We proceeded to the temple.

-The air feels different here.

-Describe it to me, Ramsay.

-It feels like the air after a spring shower, but only stronger and more penetrating.

-Discard your cigarette.

I tossed it into the sand behind me so that it would land outside the temple's perimeter. We stopped at what I guessed to be the center of the now invisible temple; both of us were silent as we stood perfectly still...and heard it: it was not unlike the heartbeat of a small child or an old man. Without warning, it stopped. It was gone so quickly that I was physically startled. Had I actually heard anything?

The air that had been so refreshing was now stifling hot as if it were noon. I could barely breathe.

-Concentrate on what lies beneath your feet and, then, tell me what you see and feel... tell me what you know, Ramsay.

I shot Jeffrey a dirty glance, but I did as I was told. I released all thoughts and tried to release myself from my body. I wanted to rid myself of physical awareness. My body would be my anchor of the greatest strength without the weight of gravity to restrict it.

My surroundings became hazy and I could see a form drifting beneath the earth and slipping down between the sand and the rubble. In the next instant, I beheld an underground chamber whose only source of light was from a strange fire placed in the center of the room. The flickering light played tricks of shadows on the chamber's walls and ceiling; it was a bizarre effect. There were symbols and pictures everywhere on the walls and, if I could guess, I would have said they were an ancient form of hieroglyphics.

I made my way around that strange and colorful room when the wall split itself open to reveal a tunnel. I entered and the walls slammed shut behind me, but not before I felt the presence of someone. Was this person a heartless priest who would torture me before delivering the death blow? An ancient priest's cruelty was matched only by his knowledge of secrets.

The tunnel was winding in about itself like some serpent...would it never end? It did end as I came out into another great chamber filled with fire and incense. I saw that a priest was praying near a fire. He looked up and beckoned me over to him. He was wearing the robe of a priest and his head was closely shaved. Was he a friend or an enemy? How could he stand the heat and the incense?

I knelt down next to him. His arm movements were precise as he stirred...something. I looked down into the color of red. I had expected to see flames, but there were none to be seen. His instrument stirred the color of red but there were no ripples.

I gazed down into the pool of red stillness and the color began to change and grow dark...so dark that it seemed as if a black hole had opened up before my eyes; a hole which reached down into the very center of the earth. It was frightening because it was so real; and I was afraid to bend forward any further for fear of falling through the black abyss.

As my fear almost paralyzed me, a speck of light appeared in the blackness; a sphere of the purest white: it was a point of light in the black nothingness. It grew and spread evenly over the purity of stillness. And, then, in a blinding burst of light, it exploded, no longer able to contain its ambition. Clusters of galaxies formed about the once still point of light which remained intact.

And, then, the galaxies began to fall back upon the light...faster and faster and faster...

I screamed.

-Ramsay, are you all right?

-Now, I am.

I was back in my body.

-Come, we must get back to the car. You can tell me everything on the way back to the city, if you feel up to it.

My murdering husband was always the gentleman.

We pulled away from the ancient ruin and Jeffrey and I began our journey back to the hotel. He drove quickly but not recklessly. I sat back and applied my make-up and told him everything. I spoke as an historian should record the events of history with dispassion. Jeffrey offered no opinion.

We returned to New York the next day.

BOOK II
JULIETTA

WHEN MY life really began with Jeffrey, I saw very little of him. Much of my time was spent with my Aunt Francesca and Kenjiro who tutored me in the ways of the occult arts. Every Friday and Sunday evening, the group met and performed rituals of differing goals. Each Sunday the mass was held and I was trained in the sacred role of the priestess. There was much detail involved and, always, I felt a veiled urgency in my training and in all of our activities.

For the next ten years, I lived within a time structure that knew little flexibility. However, that was soon to change and my life would be thrown into disruption.

When did the killings begin? I was leaving our house that early afternoon of a cloudy and hot Friday. Refusing the driver's offer of a ride, I walked in the hot air toward the midtown area. I was wearing a light, cotton summer dress and carried only a small shoulder bag with me.

I glanced back at the house and noticed how quiet and discreet it was in its dark setting: a brownstone with black bars on every window and black, iron doors that were cleverly disguised to look unobtrusive. I loved this house and enjoyed staying within it almost to the exclusion of venturing outside. Today, I felt a differently. I felt compelled to walk in the open air underneath the heavy cloud cover which would surely pour down rain at any moment.

When I reached Times Square, I made a sharp turn to my right and walked down the crowded movie section: movie houses were crammed along either side of the street and the small eateries were crowded with people. I chose a movie house and bought a ticket without even knowing what was playing and not even caring.

It was dark inside, even in the small candy concession area where I found myself browsing for something to snack on. Nothing within the glass case even so much as tempted my indulgence. I was about to go in to see the movie when a candy machine in an even darker corner caught my attention. I stooped to look at the selection and ran my finger along the red knobs which one had to pull out in order to get the candy. Indecision. I was torn between two selections until a female hand reached over and pulled a red knob and, then, placed the dime in the palm of my hand. Startled, I turned to have a look at this stranger.

-Forgive me for taking that liberty; but, I saw you hesitate and I already knew what I wanted. These "Milkshake" bars are quite delicious. Are you annoyed?

-No. But, I am just a little surprised to see the familiarity in this country. In Spain, it would be considered quite natural and even well mannered.

-Interesting that you should mention Spain. I've just spent some time there. I've spent a great deal of time there. Are we speaking too loud? I don't want to disturb the other patrons. Although, I don't imagine there are very many.

-I don't think we're speaking too loud at all.

-Let me introduce myself: I am Julietta Tebaldi.

-I'm Ramsay Bast. And-

-Yes? Ramsay, if I may, you were about to say?

-You knew that I would be coming here, didn't you?

-I had a strong feeling that you might so I followed you. Come, let us go into the theatre proper and talk. Get yourself a "Milkshake" bar. They're delicious.

Julietta had on a white and black polka dot dress which was very becoming to her lithe figure. Her hair was jet black with bangs on the side that was carelessly tossed about for effect. Her make-up was impeccable and it brought out her handsome features: the high cheekbones and the full mouth and those dark eyes. I couldn't say how old she was...not yet.

The two of us sat down in the last row of the theater and, for a moment, we were silent. The movie that was playing was some stupidity that a young teenage boy would have enjoyed taking his girlfriend to see. I unwrapped my candy bar.

-Good?

-Yes. It reminds me of something which is lighter in shade.

-Ramsay, I'll be honest with you; so much easier to be honest for one has little difficulty in retrieving unaltered facts.

-Did my husband arrange this meeting?

-I like you because you get straight to the heart of the matter.

-Do you see this little pendant I'm wearing?

-Yes.

-A cat made of a platinum alloy or so Jeffrey says.

-It's quite beautiful and quite valuable, I would imagine.

-I took it to a jeweler for insurance purposes the other day without telling Jeffrey. The jeweler was unable to classify the metal. He assumed it to be a lost artifact which had been created by an unknown craft. My husband has many secrets. Do you know Jeffrey?

-You guess the truth easily.

-It was an easy guess. So, tell me why my husband wanted us to meet here today.

-It's my belief that he wanted us to get to know each other outside of his usual group of friends.

-I've never seen you there. When did you stop coming and don't you miss the ritual mass? I would.

-I stopped going to them a very long time ago. And, in answer to your other question, I don't miss them. Let me tell my story to you, Ramsay. Jeffrey and I are old friends and we share a great many interests.

-You still correspond?

-Of course. It's imperative that we keep in contact. And, now, that you've completed the circuit all twelve of us are in contact.

-Twelve?

-I don't know how much you know or what you've been told. I assume you don't know as much as you'd like. I am an occultist and high priestess. I've studied both the black arts and the weapons of white magic. I live in total solitude except for the occasional visitors...and I have lived for a long time...predating your civilization's recorded history.

Julietta paused for a moment and, then, continues.

-Solitude and the weapons of magic have been vital to my survival on this world. I have been acquainted with the Pharaoh-gods of ancient Egypt. Look at me, Ramsay. They still live! And, even some of the ancient priests still roam in freedom: a pity about that for they are quite dangerous. How I loathe them!

-I met a priest, in a way.

-I know. He allowed you to approach him and witness the end...or the beginning, if you prefer.

-Is that so unusual?

-It is.

-Why is that?

-They're dangerous. I've already told you this. Anyway-

-Jeffrey once mentioned "superiors" to me; did he mean these priests?

-He didn't mean them. Let me continue; my main purpose in this life is to learn and prepare myself for what is soon to come.

-What is soon to come?

-I will not presume to tell you. However, Ramsay, listen closely to what I'll now tell you. You have still to meet one more member of our group of twelve: his name is Carmino; at least, it's the name that he's currently using. I don't know when he'll make himself known to you. I only hope that he's prudent about it, for seldom is he prudent about anything. Still, you may like him.

-Why haven't I met this Carmino yet?

-He's a loner, like myself. And, for him, also, it's not necessary to partake of the ritual on a regular basis.

-Wouldn't Jeffrey prefer to have you all with him in one location?

-He wouldn't. You still don't know your husband very well, do you?

-Do you?

-I've known him longer and...you may want to ask him about Carmino. You have a right to know about him.

Julietta took a bit of her candy bar and continued.

-Ramsay, your life right now seems ordered and structured, and that is how one's life should be. But, very soon, the murders will begin- let me finish! When the last murder has occurred, you and Mark must meet and bring about the impossible. Pay careful attention to the details of each funeral: each coffin must be hermetically sealed and under no circumstances must any embalming be done. Say that you hear everything I tell you.

-Yes, Julietta, I hear you, but in God's name-

-Oh? I wasn't aware that there was a single god. How amusing and stupid.

-Will you die?

-No. Carmino will also be spared. However, neither one of us will be able to help you and Mark. Enemies will abound, though, and quite frankly I don't know how you'll be able to avoid them, but you must. Our enemies' strength lies in their cunning and their unspeakable cruelty.

-Why will Mark and I be spared?

-Ask Jeffrey that question. I must leave soon.

-How old is Jeffrey?

-He is a young man, of course. Do you need me to tell you this?

-I think he's older than he claims he is. I think they all are, except for my Aunt Francesca.

-Indeed. Don't take anything for granted about your aunt. Mark is young and so are you, and that's all that matters. You lived once before in ancient Alexandria, and we knew each other quite well.

-How do you know that people will be murdered?

-It's been foretold. I must leave now. We'll share a cab. And, Ramsay, don't walk the streets alone anymore, there are too many dangers in this world and others.

BOOK III
THE CARDS

CHAPTER VII
FRANCESCA

I FUMBLED in my bag for the door key, but the door was already opened.

-Oh! I didn't know you had come, Aunt Francesca.

I kissed her on the cheek.

-I only just got here and dear Kenjiro was keeping me company.

-Kenjiro is here, also? Anybody else? We could start a party.

-Do not be impertinent, Ramsay; come in out of the rain.

How generous of her to invite me into my own home. I threw my hair back and shook some of the rain out of it and followed my aunt into the drawing room where Kenjiro had helped himself to some of the brandy. Kenjiro was always a welcome guest and, of course, our possessions were his.

Kenjiro addressed me.

-I hope you don't mind my intrusion, but I must see Jeffrey and I must also speak to you, Ramsay.

I sat down on the sofa and Kenjiro brought me over a brandy. Aunt Francesca sat down next to me telling me that I looked tired. I didn't feel tired.

-Kenjiro, what can I do for you?

-I brought you a present.

It was a small, wooden box which appeared to have no lid.

-Kenjiro, I'm very bad at opening trick boxes so you'd better show me how it's done.

He placed his index finger on one of its four corners and the lid sprang open to reveal a pack of Tarot cards.

-Don't take them out no. You must wait until I'm gone.

-Do it now for your aunt, Ramsay. I am bursting with curiosity!

-Not while I'm here! Please respect my wishes on this matter, Francesca.

I assured him that I wouldn't even take the cards out of the box until he was through with his business with Jeffrey and long gone. He showed me how to close the box while removing it from my Aunt Francesca's gaze.

For half an hour, the three of us talked about domestic matters and how they should be kept in order. I heard Jeffrey's footsteps in the hallway and stopped talking. My husband never used the front entrance; it was always by way of the side entrance that he came in. He came to the door and nodded gravely to us. For a moment, his eyes rested upon the box that I still held in my hand. He gave Kenjiro a sharp and disapproving look and, then, beckoned him out into the hallway.

-What was that all about?

-You're asking me? I don't know my husband at all. I never have. And, you, dear Aunt Francesca, do I know you at all?

I got up and paced about the room. Before my aunt could reply, a flash of lightning struck.

-My God, that frightened me!

-Oh? Is there only one God?

-What are you saying, Ramsay?

-A strange woman set me straight on that score to-day. Yes. I see you know whom I mean and don't bother to deny it.

-Do not speak to your aunt in that tone of voice.

-My aunt? I don't know who you are, only who you say you are.

-Stop this!

-You know what I should do? I should tell your fortune now and ask the cards who is this woman who drew me into a marriage and a life that as yet have no reason. Maybe, the cards will give me a few answers?

My aunt slapped me hard in the face.

-Enough!

-I'm sorry...forgive me, Aunt Francesca.

I rubbed that side of my face.

-Come and sit down and calm yourself. I will pour you some more brandy and, then, I will leave. Tell my fortune when I am gone and the fortunes of us all. Promise your aunt that you will do that.

-I will.

My Aunt Francesca was the first to die. I was in my drawing room sipping brandy and turning over the dreaded Tarot cards. Were they Tarot cards? I'd never seen a deck like it before: it was composed of PRIESTS and PRIESTESSES, THE CAT and MOUSE GAME, THE KILLER BLADE, THE HANGED MAN, THE MATADOR OF BLOOD, SHATTERED GLASS, THE ICE QUEEN, THE HOUSE OF NO DOORS AND WINDOWS, THE PHYSICIAN, FUN and GAMES, LIGHTNING and THUNDER, and THE BLANK CARD, FEAR, DECEIT, DREAD, and THE SAMURAI and more disturbing cards.

No instructions came with the box; an absurd thought and it made me want to laugh. The spread was simplicity, itself: a circle composed of five cards with a sixth card in the center which was the card of destiny.

The rain and the thunder continued and the drawing room grew dark. I reached over and switched on the small lamp to give me just enough light to see by. I shuffled the deck slowly and carefully and, then, cut it and placed the top half on the other pile. I turned over the first card and the circle began to build itself.

THE PRIESTESS: THE RULER AND THE RULED

My Aunt Francesca was in her own home now. She was sitting at her desk and writing out her correspondence. I could actually see her; it was like looking into a painting and seeing life instilled within it.

-How tiresome to keep up all this correspondence. And, to think that at one time, I had a secretary to do all this for me.

I never knew of my aunt having a secretary. What else didn't I know? She folded her last letter and slipped it into an envelope. Even she is guided by the light of only one lamp while the rest of her parlor is in darkness.

-To think of the length of my life and all the identities that I have had to assume. I should have been more like Julietta, a recluse, that one. But, even she has had to assume more identities than one can point at. I do not like her at all.

The lightning lit up the room and the thunder sent a not so very pleasant vibration through the house. She went over to the sideboard to pour herself another drink. She happened to glance over at the sofa and saw that no one was sitting there. Why did that thought even occur to her? All the doors and windows were locked so what was there to fear?

My aunt brought her drink over to the writing table and sat down...again, glancing back at the sofa. The sofa was empty. Who would be on it?

LIGHTNING and THUNDER

-Why am I so unsettled? I am alone and it is how I choose to be. Jeffrey approves and I need no one else's approval.

She played with the sealed envelopes on the table and, finally, put them into one neat pile. She reached into the top drawer and drew out a very sharp and heavy letter opener. She tapped her brandy glass with its sharp point.

THE PRIEST

On Aunt Francesca's writing table was a photograph of Jeffrey which she had placed in a silver frame a long time ago.

-It is he who rescued me from the obscurity all those long years ago. Penniless and dying, I wandered the streets of Barcelona until he came and lifted me up from my misery. My beautiful Jeffrey! I love him and will always be loyal to him. But, his enemies frighten me so. I can feel their presence always and, yet, tonight they are concealing their presence from me. I know they are here!

Again, she turned to look at the still empty sofa.

THE PRIEST OF DECEIT

-Enough of this! No! I must have no more wine or I will not be able to sleep. If I am to be murdered, let them murder me in my bed.

As Aunt Francesca got up from the writing table, she took the letter opener with her and left the empty brandy glass behind. She glanced around the room and switched off the lamp just as lightning struck and the thunder exploded like some horrible man-made weapon. On the sofa was a man staring at her with black eyes crazed with madness...the madness and cunning of calculation.

My Aunt Francesca screamed and ran toward the door; but, the priest was on top of her in a moment. She tried to plunge the letter opener into his black heart.

PRIEST OF DREAD

-I have no heart.

The voice was sweet, but the breath stank of decay. My aunt gasped and dropped her weapon to the floor as he dragged her over to the couch. He pinned her arms to the couch and drew from his robe a long, thin blade that I knew had to be heavily coated with poison. On the end of the blade was a sharp coil of gold that when withdrawn with each thrust brought torture as it ripped and shredded the flesh.

The priest thrust it into her stomach and slowly withdrew it. My aunt's agonized cries could be heard over the thunder. He thrust it into her pelvis and twisted the blade before he withdrew it.

-Ramsay!

At that moment, I understood what I had to do...what must be done. He thrust the blade into my aunt's body once more being careful not to pierce any vital organ lest the release of death deprive him of his filthy sport.

The sofa was becoming soaked with blood and my aunt was slowly losing consciousness. Her murderer was aware of this and decided to strike the death blow. With a strong and quick thrust, he plunged the blade through her chest and...my aunt died on the blood soaked couch. The priest put his weapon back into his robe and disappeared into the darkness.

THE BLANK CARD

CHAPTER VIII
KENJIRO

THE NEXT morning, Jeffrey called on my Aunt Francesca knowing full well what had happened to her. He let himself in and walked directly into the parlor. The first thing he saw was her body. He ran to it and held it tightly, praying and crying and cursing; praying for her soul, crying for her physical death, and cursing the filth who had done this to her

He straightened himself up and walked over to the phone. He picked up the receiver with one hand and with the other he lifted the empty brandy glass and smashed it against the table. He dialed his own phone number...and I? I answered the phone.

-Ramsay?

-Yes, Jeffrey? What should I do?

-Prepare my surgical room and then call the mortuary and see to the arrangements. Ask Kenjiro and Allyson to get in touch with the others. They will be needed for the funeral. I grieve for your aunt.

-Thank you. I'll see to everything.

I put down the receiver. I wasn't even crying.

Jeffrey and our chauffeur moved my aunt's body to the surgical room and my husband set to work repairing my aunt's body.

The funeral was held the next day and all of us were present, including some of my family members. Afterward, a repast was given for the mourners and when my last family member had departed, the nine of us held an informal meeting in the drawing room.

-Is this the beginning of it, then? Do we all wait and take our turns to be slaughtered like pigs? Answer me, Jeffrey, please. It's Armando speaking to you. You're our leader, so you should tell us what to do. A leader should lead, or am I speaking out of turn?

-Were the police notified, Jeffrey?

-No, Tana. They could be of no help and no one was to touch Francesca's body. The appropriate lies were told to Ramsay's family; that she suffered a stroke.

He drained his brandy glass while all the time looking at no one. I refilled his glass. Not even a thank you.

-Yes, Armando, it has begun. It was foretold a long time ago and it is all part of the process of life, so to speak.

-To be slaughtered, Kenjiro? Is that what you're telling us?

-Yes. If you must put it so indelicately. And, you, my friend, make me wonder about your apparent unpreparedness for the event. Fear will only worsen it.

-Besides, we will have the revenge, won't we, Ramsay?

-I'm no opponent to revenge, Timothy.

-Good girl! I had a feeling that you wouldn't be.

-Oh? What do you mean by that?

-It's a compliment, Ramsay, of rather high grade.

Mark stood in his usual corner; all of his bandages had been removed, except for one long horizontal one which covered the bridge of his nose. Lisa was leaning on the drinks table; already she was on her third drink.

-Did the dear girl suffer so dreadfully?

-Yes, Lisa. But, not for as long as my aunt's murderer would have liked.

-So, dear Ramsay, it's to be torture first and then the old death blow. It's the torture part that makes my skin crawl. Who's next? No- don't tell me. I don't want to know.

-I understand that we have to die, but must we be pawns of their cruel game? There are only twelve of them and they want to take our place-

-Careful of what you say, Allyson. Well, Mark, Mr. Silent Man, nothing to tell us or add to our worry? Speak, you bastard! Speak to Armando!

Mark slapped Armando hard in the face. As all of us turned to stare, Armando backed off, holding his hand to his face.

Jeffrey spoke to the group.

-Enough of this! There is no more to be said here, tonight. We must all continue with our studies and our work and be prepared. Keep your houses in order. You may leave now if you wish.

Everyone in the drawing room left with the exception of me and Jeffrey. I went to the sideboard and poured us both another brandy. I offered Jeffrey the glass.

-Thank you, Ramsay. Black is your color; you should wear it, always.

-After last night, I may. But, tell me, Jeffrey, when will the last of us be killed?

-Are you looking forward that much to my own death? You've never forgiven me for that cretin's death in Egypt, have you?

-I'm not through thinking about it, if that's what you mean. Would you answer my question, please?

-Probably within ten years' time. I will be their last victim. Disappointed, my sweet?

-You make me out to be so cruel. I'm not; and I will always be faithful to you.

-Are you taking an oath now? Be careful, you may outgrow it. Ramsay, when will you give another reading?

-Soon.

-Whose destiny will you intrude upon?

-Is that what I'm doing? In that case, I won't do any more readings. I'll give the cards back to Kenjiro.

-Don't be angry. In a sense, the cards are your protection.

-Maybe I don't want to be protected.

-Don't be flippant with me.

-Why were you upset with Kenjiro the other day for giving them to me?

-Francesca was not to have seen them. No one else is to know about them, do you understand that? A simple "yes" will do for an answer.

-Yes.

-Good. In due time, I'll tell them of their existence. Now, when is your next reading?

-Tonight.

-Whose destiny will you intrude upon?

-Kenjiro.

-Why?

-Because of his knowledge of the cards. I must punish us both for that.

-I'll leave you to your work.

He lit a cigarette and left the room. I took a hold of the small wooden box and pressed down on its corner. I took out the deck and shuffled the cards.

Kenjiro was at his school where he gave lessons in self-defense and the art of meditation.

THE SAMURAI

Kenjiro walked across the polished, wooden floor wearing his black kimono of fine silk. The walls had no adornments on them and the ceiling, painted black for the illusion of depth, contained only the barest of light fixtures. With even and majestic strides, he walked the perimeter of the room completely aware of all that was around him. His bare feet touched the floor gently but with firmness for even a casual walk for this man was a work of art.

The room was hot, but his walk stirred a breeze within the folds of his kimono. The incense filled the air and he breathed in the soothing vapors. The room was in darkness, but the Master had the eyes of a cat.

THE SAMURAI

Around Kenjiro's waist was a leather strap and in its holster was a sword of stainless steel. It was of recent make and it had been made according to Master Kenjiro's most exacting instructions. He held the hilt of it tightly in his hand as he was looking into the dark...looking for an enemy whom he wanted to confront. He was not afraid. He had conquered his fear of physical pain and death.

PRIEST OF DEATH

-Come for me, unseen woman who gives birth to Man. I know you. To give form is to give limitation and the humble whisper of a man's longings. Come for me.

THE KILLER BLADE: A SWORD FOR ONE'S SELF AND A SWORD FOR ONE'S ENEMY

-I see eyes flashing in the darkness. The night outside is clear and the full moon and the stars can be seen overhead. The air is still and warm. I love the fight. I will come to you priests of death as a warrior should...as a warrior should die!

He leaped toward the two priests, but as they saw him coming, they leapt apart. However, Kenjiro was too well trained not to anticipate this and, with one quick move, he veered to his right and cut down his enemy.

The priest's blood splashed against the wall as his decapitated head went flying through the air, smashing into the opposite wall.

Kenjiro charged toward the other priest, but this priest sidestepped him and, for a moment, Kenjiro lost his footing. A priest grabbed his right arm and tried to wrench his sword from him. Then, another priest grabbed his left arm as a third priest came toward him. Four of them had been dispatched to do this deed.

As the third priest came running toward Kenjiro, dagger in hand, Kenjiro sent him a hard kick to the chest. The priest fell backward and his back was slammed against the floor breaking it. One of the two priests holding Kenjiro managed to get hold of his own dagger and slit Kenjiro's throat. Of course, the priest's dagger was poisonous in order to enhance the death blow.

Kenjiro broke loose and scooped up his own sword. He was dying and he knew it.

THE SAMURAI

Kenjiro ran to the corner of the room, but no one was following him. The other two priests, who had survived, stayed their ground and dared not attack. Kenjiro placed his sword in the corner of the room, upright, and with all his strength, he plunged himself on to the weapon. He died instantly. The priest's poisoned dagger had not killed him.

THE BLANK CARD

I knew that Jeffrey was standing outside the drawing room listening to the sound of each card being placed on the table. My husband took a last drag on his cigarette, and I asked him to come in.

-Are we to arrange everything as before?

-Yes. I'll go to Kenjiro now.

-Did he have any relatives?

-None. We were his family.

-Why can't I cry? I couldn't even cry for my Aunt Francesca.

-Save your tears for me, Ramsay.

CHAPTER IX
ALLYSON

-WHAT A talent I have for unfolding death.

-That's an almost accurate statement, Ramsay. However, your description deserves much more detail.

-I think I'll put my cards away for the moment; two funerals back to back are trying for even the most dedicated of followers. Nerves will be a little tense at Kenjiro's wake, don't you think, Jeffrey?

-What are you smiling about?

-Nothing. There's nothing to smile about. I have nothing to smile about.

-Nevertheless, you are smiling and at my expense.

-I'm not laughing at you.

-Good. It wouldn't be a nice thing to do. Tell me this: who are you?

-I beg your pardon?

-Who are you? Tell me.

-At the moment, dear husband, I feel just a bit like Madame deFarge in the French Revolution, knitting her prophecies of doom. It's my gift to the group; your group.

-Your talents go beyond that, Ramsay. You're gifted and your powers-

-Tell me about them, if you don't mind.

-The power of prophecy and, of course, resurrection; is that clear enough for you?

-It'll have to be.

-So...who are you?

I leaned forward in my chair wanting to throw my drink in his face.

-I should take out the cards again and read every-one's fortune and be done with it; except yours, Jeffrey, I'll let you linger. But, all of that is no good, is it? I'm nothing, so how can nothing hurt anyone?

-Perhaps.

-Perhaps, what?

-Lower your voice, please, Ramsay. Loud words aren't necessary; perhaps, words aren't even necessary.

-Oh? Can you read my mind? How talented of you to know what's going on in my mind. I'd like to know what's going on in your mind. So, tell me, what am I thinking?

-You're in love with Mark.

He lit another cigarette and took quite a deep drag on it.

-Why don't you just swallow it?

-Cigarette?

-Thank you.

-You're in love with Mark. Not denying it, are we? Should I admire you for that, Ramsay? Or, perhaps, I should detest you and him and your silence.

-The love is platonic.

-Carefully chosen and truthful words. Thank you. I don't mind the two of you loving each other platonically. It amounts to nothing.

-I so rarely hear him speak; why is that?

-He's a man of a few words who knows the power of them. Mark came to me. I did not find him.

-When and where did he find you?

He was lying to me, but I decided to be civilized and play the game.

-You don't hide your interest. Just before the outbreak of the Second World War at his gymnasium. Why did he approach me? His intuitive sense told him to. And, I recognized his potential at once. Does that satisfy your curiosity?

-I'm surprised you told me that much.

-Take a break from your cards and let's attend to Kenjiro's funeral arrangements; would you mind so much?

-Not at all. I was going to say that it would take my mind off things, but how could it?

Another year of darkness passed. It filled my life with boredom and periods of activity, but never with any real satisfaction. I existed as did my husband and his friends. Every weekend we would meet for our ritual and, then, our mass would follow. I was the priestess, always. Jeffrey, Armando, Timothy, and Mark would take their turns as the priest, each unique and fascinating in his own way. Allyson, Tana, and Lisa seemed to enjoy the part of the deacon doing a superb job of it.

I saw no more of Julietta and her mannequin-like personae. And, Carmino...who was he, this mystery man?

-You wouldn't like him.

-Why wouldn't I like him?

-He's not your type of man or friend.

-Oh? Is there to be a choice between the two? I can't have male friends? But, I do, Jeffrey.

-Do you?

-She has, Jeffrey.

-Are you my wife's friend, Armando?

-If one went by your tone of voice, Jeffrey, the answer would have to be no.

-And, you, Timothy?

-Leave me out of your domestic scraps, old man.

We were once again in the drawing room. I watched Allyson pacing the room with her untouched drink in her hand. Lisa was also watching her. Tana was watching Lisa.

-Allyson would you please stop that pacing? I do believe that you're driving our Lisa quite insane.

-Rather.

-I'm sorry, Tana. I didn't think anyone was taking any notice. I'm sorry.

Allyson sat down in a chair at the far corner of the room and stared at her drink. Timothy walked over and offered her a cigarette which she refused.

-What's with her?

-I really don't know, Lisa. Well, maybe, I do.

-I loathe Sunday evenings. I shouldn't because I don't work, but I suppose it's a force of habit. The evening should be stretched out as long as possible.

-I know what you mean. But, I do enjoy the quiet of a Sunday evening; there's a stillness that hovers in the air of things having been completed and-

-Ramsay?

-Yes, Jeffrey?

-We were discussing Carmino.

-But, the subject isn't appealing to you so why not drop it?

-As you wish.

-I haven't seen Julietta in a long time; so very enigmatic. Does anyone know anything about her?

-I believe Ramsay was the last to see her, Tana. Isn't that right, Ramsay? It was at a rather sleazy movie theatre.

-I don't know, Jeffrey. I saw her a year ago on the afternoon of my aunt's death. Come to think of it, quite a lot happened that day.

-Funny, that: I don't believe in coincidences, do you? There must be a connection.

-Isn't everything connected one way or another, Lisa?

-You know what I mean, Ramsay, dear...between Julietta's appearance, your aunt's and Kenjiro's murders and those lovely cards you play with. Don't tell my fortune.

The box of cards was on the table in front of me; everyone now knew about them. I leaned forward in my chair and picked it up.

-Oh, no!

-Don't worry, Tana, I won't tell your fortune...not today. I'll tell Allyson's fortune.

The room became very quiet. Allyson got up and, still holding on to her glass, crossed the room to where I sat.

-I'm leaving. Don't anyone follow me.

I don't believe anyone was about to. The girl gathered up her things and left.

I opened the box of cards.

THE ICE QUEEN

Allyson walked to the corner and attempted to hail a passing cab. After a long minute, she was successful.

-The Downtown Ice Rink, please.

The cab driver sped on like some madman causing several small accidents along the way; but, both he and Allyson arrived at the rink unharmed. It was already well past midnight and that part of town was even more desolate than it usually was over the weekend.

Allyson rummaged through her bag to find the money to pay the cab driver.

-I'm sorry this is taking so long.

No answer.

Where was her wallet? She'd had it with her when she left.

-Having difficulty?

The sound of the voice was cultured and cynical. The intonation didn't slip by Allyson. She looked up with fear in her eyes.

In the darkness of the cab, the driver turned his head and took off his cap. Allyson screamed and threw her bag into his face the face of a priest. She jumped out of the car and ran into the rink.

PRIEST OF DEATN: THE EDGE OF A DREAM

Once inside the rink, she bolted the door behind her and ran to the locker room slamming this door shut. Quickly and breathlessly, she undressed and changed into her body leotard and put on her skates. Her hands trembled and she had difficulty tightening the laces at each loop.

-Please!

Finally, it was done. Allyson went to the double doors to open them and to escape on to the ice; but, the blade of a sword plunged its way through the slit and the point of it nearly caught her. She turned to run and tripped over the blade of her skate. She broke her fall with her left hand. In agony, she screamed, but managed to get up.

SHATTERED GLASS

Groping her way into the bathroom, Allyson tried switching on the light. She leaned against the cold and dirty tiles and carefully touched her left arm. It felt like a fracture. She knew this because she had injured herself once before in like manner, but that had been at the beginning of her career and it had taken place where it should have, on the ice.

Allyson noticed that the light from a street lamp was filtering through the bathroom's filthy window. She went to the window and tried to open it, but it was jammed shut. She could hear the blade sliding through the double doors just a few feet away...sliding and scratching and picking at the lock. She walked over to the sink and stared for a moment at her reflection in the mirror: tears were streaming down her lovely face...suddenly, the glass shattered and fell to the floor.

THE PRIEST

The lock of the double doors clicked open and eight priests walked into the room. They made their way toward Allyson.

THE PHANTOM OF RECOLLECTION

They walked into the bathroom chanting and murmuring and avoiding a patch of light on the floor. They formed a circle and didn't seem to notice Allyson. She thought of taking her own life. The shattered glass...

Now the priests took notice of her. The patch of light vanished from the room. The priests grabbed Allyson and killed her...each of them driving a piece of shattered mirror into her body...dispassionately.

Allyson's life leapt before her eyes. Her novice years as a skater and her years of maturity and grace filled with triumph and pain and frustration. Her love of the ice and the glorious freedom of movement across its surface like a beautiful swan gliding across the still and unbroken surface of the water...skimming the fabric of the lake's reflected cover. Soaring like the dove...quietly and with purity of movement and form...precise movement of limb and body...precise movement of limb and body...

The murderers fled.

THE BLANK CARD

CHAPTER X
ARMANDO

THE MORNING sun laid bare the slaughter of the previous night's work. The police found Jeffrey's name in Allyson's locker and informed him of the murder. All of us were in the drawing room with the cards still on the table. I had just turned over the last card.

-Ramsay? Put them away, please.

-Just maybe, Ramsay was having too much fun with them, Jeffrey..

-That's being cynical, Lisa; but, it suits you.

-Thank you for defending me, Timothy.

-Enough. I'll go to the police and claim the body.

-The police might become suspicious of us. I'm worried, Jeffrey.

-Why, Tana, we have air tight alibis? Armando, coming with me?

-True. I never thought of that.

Allyson's body was brought to our place and, as had become the custom, Jeffrey made the necessary repairs before public interment.

I'll answer the question for you: Armando was next and he knew it. He was calmer than I thought he would be: calmer in one sense, but excited in another. It was his sexual excitement that had been aroused and he made no secret of this.

It was the Sunday following Allyson's murder that he made the announcement to us all. Bear in mind, it was 1958 and there were certain things that one didn't dare allude to in public even among the best of friends.

Armando spoke:

-Take your cards out, Ramsay, and tell the hour of my death. Kenjiro didn't give those cards to you to play solitaire with. I think I hate you more than anyone here! But, I'll tell you something: I love Jeffrey. Yes! Look at the queer, the pansy, the homosexual! I don't deny it! What would be the fucking point? But, don't worry Ramsay.

I wasn't worried.

-Jeffrey won't have me. I've offered myself. I've bared my soul and he rejected me.

-Perhaps, dear boy, one of those ghastly priests will have you?

-That was unkind, Lisa.

-Sorry, Jeffrey.

-Your time will come, bitch! I leave you all now. I need to find a partner for one last, good lay.

Armando slammed the door behind him.

-I hope someone manages to put a smile on his face. Good riddance to him. Who do you all look at me? I've said what we're all thinking, is that not so?

Tana looked over at Mark who was neither laughing nor smiling and this irritated her. No one denied it; although, Mark could have.

I took out the box of cards and laid out the entire spread, except for the blank card which I held in my right hand. For a moment, I was startled at the spread...one card was repeated four times...a card that was not easy to look at.

THE HOUSE OF NO DOORS AND WINDOWS

True to his word, Armando had gone seeking the enjoyment of sex with another man. The place he chose was on the Lower East Side of Manhattan in a brownstone that had been converted into a "bathhouse."

Armando was lying naked on a cot in a cubicle. His manhood was being massaged by a young man who was taking too long with the blow job. Impatiently, Armando grabbed the young man by the nape of the neck and shoved his mouth down to the base of his penis. Armando reached orgasm.

-Get out.

The young man skulked out of the tiny room; lucky for him.

Armando got off the cot; but, he was still hard even though he was no longer excited. I've never understood this in men. He was angry now, but at himself and not others. He wanted to leave this place, but to go where? He paced about in the room with the one red bulb: it seems that that color is universally used. He pounded his fist into his right palm, still naked and still with a throbbing erection. Even he was beginning to get impatient for the thing to go down.

The door opened.

MATADOR OF BLOOD
MATADOR OF BLOOD
MATADOR OF BLOOD
MATADOR OF BLOOD

-I've been expecting you.

The priests grabbed him and laid him out on the cot. One priest held down his legs while another sat on his chest and pinned back his arms. The third did the deed. He grabbed a hold of Armando's manhood and withdrew from his cloak a vial of clear liquid. Carefully, he placed the vial's lip to the small opening of Armando's penis and poured its contents down the shaft.

The three priests left him to die in excruciating agony. The poison crept inside his body and went straight to every vital organ. Armando writhed in agony on the cot while the acid spread throughout...burning his insides...rendering him senseless one moment and, then, conscious the next until his body heaved the death rattle.

THE BLANK CARD

When Armando was found, he was still erect.

The priests were cruel.

CHAPTER XI
TANA

-I WANT my death to be now.

-I don't understand you, Timothy. I thought you were the kind of man who lived life to the fullest. I really thought that you, of all people, would want the most time. Let me give you the most time, as much as I can. You'll be second only to Jeffrey.

-You're too generous, Mrs. Bast. Give me a card reading now, if you please.

-For God's sake, be reasonable, Timothy. We've only just interred Allyson and Armando and there simply can't be another funeral so bloody soon. The police will really think we did it. Talk about your ghastly ironies!

-Lisa is right. Is there absolutely no other way? Jeffrey, darling, must we all die; and to be murdered by those priests with their foul smell of death?

-There is no other way, Tana.

-If Timothy is to die next then who- I don't want to know. I only pray that I have the courage of Kenjiro to kill myself.

-Perhaps Mark will have that courage, Tana?

Mark stood there and drank his whiskey.

-We must wait a few years, Timothy.

-No, Jeffrey.

-The police are suspicious enough as it is.

-Perhaps, they could help us.

-Tana, I didn't think you were a fool; perhaps, after all, you are.

-Jeffrey, stop laughing!

-Sorry, Ramsay, but really...

-Stop it! Tana is a guest in our house. I won't have you making her an object of ridicule.

Jeffrey stopped laughing. He was smoking heavily in those days of stress.

There was a knock on the door.

-Come in!

Jeffrey always snapped at the servants. There was a Miss Julietta Tebaldi to be announced. All of us stood up in undisguised shock. I switched off the main lamp, so now only one light was burning under a crimson lamp shade.

Julietta walked in with a defiant air about her; although, I don't think that was her intent. She was wearing sunglasses and was hatless, an odd sight for a chic woman of this period. Her dress and accessories were all black, and she wore very high heels.

-Julietta, what an extraordinary surprise! Please, sit down.

I watched her.

-Not just yet, Jeffrey, I wish to stand for a time. But, a refreshment would not be unwelcome.

-What may we offer you: a brandy or some coffee?

-Both. And, perhaps, some chocolates to go with them? I've grown rather found of chocolates in the past few years.

-I'll instruct the servants to purchase some immediately.

-You don't keep any in the house, Ramsay? How dreadful! Perhaps, now, you will.

I didn't smile, but Jeffrey did.

-Your own personal stash...we'll keep it available from now on.

Why do men fawn so?

Julietta sat down in one of the arm chairs most distant from the one light illuminating the room. She produced a cigarette from her purse. Timothy rushed over to offer her a light. I cast glances at Lisa and Tana. We understood each other.

-Thank you.

Timothy had fooled us; it was only for a moment that he fawned over our guest. He thrust a question at her.

-Well, Julietta, what brings you here? And, please, give a direct answer.

-To expect a direct answer from me would be demanding of you, Timothy. I don't give direct answers because I don't like them. A direct question and answer do not belong in the fabric of civilization. They leave no room for conjecture.

-Are you so damned civilized, darling?

-But, of course, Lisa, there are the few of us...and the rest have their uses.

-Such as, darling?

-Slave labor and the military who are the protectors of the core of civilization.

-Indeed!

Julietta turned her head to look in Tana's direction. I kept watching Julietta aware that she knew it. Did it amuse her, annoy her or did she simply not care? How very insulting if she didn't care. I wanted her to care. This woman was strange...bizarre. Her movements seemed postured and, yet, I'm sure they weren't.

-Ramsay?

-Yes? I'm sorry.

-How have you been?

I hadn't expected her to speak to me. It took me a few moments to recover as everyone watched and not in complete sympathy, either.

-I've been fine.

-But, you have been surrounded by death; does that suit you?

-I hope it does. There are more to come and, I seem to be at the center of it all.

-Does that repulse you?

-No.

-But, you would rather give life?

-I would much rather give life.

-It's a relief to hear you say that.

-I'll ask my question, again, Julietta. Why are you here?

-To observe Ramsay, Timothy, and to make certain that she goes on with her card readings.

Julietta smiled at me. Yes...this woman had had extensive cosmetic surgery.

-I wish to hell she'd get on with mine. End this bloody guessing game..

-You surprise me, Timothy; a full blooded Englishman, like yourself. I thought you would want to spit at death in its face when it finally overtook you. You disappoint me.

-We all feel rather the same way, love. As a matter of fact, we were just discussing it before you so casually walked in, uninvited.

-Lisa, do you insinuate that I've interrupted some private conversation?

-I don't *insinuate* anything.

Jeffrey came back into the room with our butler, who served Julietta her coffee, brandy and chocolates. My dear husband didn't offer me any, and I was quite ravenous for a piece of chocolate. I kept staring at our guest, trying to make out the person and the body that encased it. She was in deep shadows, but hadn't I sat next to her in a darkened cab and in a dark movie house?

-Enjoy the last few years, Timothy, and don't be blinded by the illusion of time for all that will soon cease, at least for a non-moment. God is about to clench his fist, again.

-Do you know him personally, Julietta?

-Don't be impertinent, Lisa. When I say "God" I mean that unity among the countless unities.

-How long has your own lifetime been just curious.

-Do you ask me my age? I won't tell you. However, the inevitable has been coming since the fall of Memphis, the last bastion of the sciences.

-That old, dear?

-Even older, Lisa. Perhaps, I even knew the creature that your misinformed Bible calls Eve.

-Why are you here, Julietta?

-I wanted you to ask me that question, Ramsay.

-Why are you here?

-How impatient you are! To tell you who must die and in what order.

Tana sprang to her feet and ran from the room. Lisa defiantly stayed where she was.

-Tana will be next.

-Damn you!

-Then, Timothy.

-Thanks.

-And, then, Lisa and...it pains me to say it...Jeffrey, my love.

-And, then, what?

Julietta leaned back in her seat and ate another chocolate. I asked her for one.

-Then, you go into hiding for a time, Ramsay. Search out this young man, Mark. The two of you will know what to do.

-We will? I'm not so sure about that.

-You were chosen for your intelligence and for your achievements in lives past. And, Timothy, think of Kenjiro and how he met his own death with dignity and bravery: two of the cornerstones of civilization.

-Are we back to civilization and its sordid components? Why are you being so damned kind?

-Kindness, Timothy, has its place in a cultured and civilized society: it is merely the subtext of an emotion. Discretion also has its place in a cultured world, for with it one keeps a check and a balance, so to speak. The years will pass like all the other years which preceded them. What is a year within the scheme of time? Nothing. I must go now

Jeffrey offered her his hand.

-Thank you. Ramsay, after you've gone into hiding, you may meet Carmino. Don't look forward to it; you won't like him.

-Why won't I like him? You're the second person to tell me this.

-The bastard enjoys the kill.

She left with Jeffrey.

-Timothy?

-Yes, Ramsay?

-Would you hand me the rest of those chocolates, please?

-Don't hog them all for yourself; hand me a few, will you?

-Timothy, give Lisa a handful.

Timothy offered Mark some chocolates, but he refused...I looked at Timothy full in the face and he knew what I was thinking...tonight was his night to die....nearly eight years to the day and we found ourselves back in the drawing room...a summer's night which held the promise of a thunder storm.

However, Tana must die first.

THE TOWER OF THE ELEMENTALS: INFINITE JOURNEY TO MEET AT THE CROSSROADS OF INFINITY.

Jeffrey sent Tana away. He allowed her the use of our chauffeur and our limousine. As the car turned the corner, it started to rain on the dry, dusty pavements. Tana stared out the window and tried not to think of any one thing; but one particular thought kept coming back.

-Stop the car, please. I wish to get out.

-But, Madame, you'll be drenched.

-Never mind that. Open the door for me.

-As you wish.

The chauffeur obeyed and Tana stepped out of the car and into the pouring rain.

-Drive off, please. Return to your master.

The chauffeur drove off and came straight back to us.

Tana made her way down the block toward a police station. Would she have betrayed us? She didn't get her chance, if that was her intention. As she stepped from the curb into the street, a hand reached up from the sewer grating and grabbed her ankle in a vise-like grip. The iron grating was flipped open and pushed aside like cardboard. She was dragged down into the sewer.

-Help me!

-There is no one here to help you.

MAN OF FORTUNE AND MISFORTUNE.

The priest lifted Tana to her feet.

-Kill me and be done with it.

-That would be a mercy.

Someone else grabbed her from behind and this cretin began to tear the clothes from her body. The priests had hired some loathsome underling to rape her..

THE PRIESTESS

Finished, he withdrew and the priest killed the cretin. Then, he looked at Tana. She spit at him.

PRIEST OF DECEIT

PRIEST OF DECAY

PRIEST OF DREAD

-Allow me to help you up.

-Keep your filthy hands off me! Where are my clothes?

-Crawl...and, perhaps, you may save yourself.

Tana did not crawl.

-Look at me, priest. Don't you want me? Break your holy vow and take me. Disrobe so that I may look upon your body, as well. You tell me no, but your manhood is responding. Feel it with your hand and tell me that it doesn't feel good. It does! Come to me, priest.

He broke his vows.
THE BLANK CARD

CHAPTER XII
TIMOTHY

OUR CHAUFFEUR returned to where he had dropped off Tana, one block further along the way. He got out of the car and looked down into the sewer. He could see nothing so, reluctantly, he had to hoist himself down. What he saw caused him to vomit: three dead corpses and two of them lying intertwined. It took him quite a while to separate the two bodies. Like Kenjiro before her, Tana had succeeded in killing off a priest.

-Timothy?

-Get on with it, Ramsay.

-Don't you want to leave? I would.

-No.

-Why not?

-I want to die here. Does that disturb you in any way? It shouldn't. I'm the one who's going to bloody die.

-Jeffrey?

-Let him stay, if he wants; although, I could have him forcibly removed.

-Don't try it, Jeffrey.

-You're placing Ramsay's life in danger. It's not to be this way.

-Damn the so-called "way!" I'm sick of this charade.

-You're getting to be rather impossible, Timothy. Leave!

-No!

-Coward.

-I'd like to see how brave you are at your time, Ramsay. Now, open the box of cards, Mrs. Bast.

-Ramsay, don't.

-I must, Jeffrey.

-Timothy, leave us, now!

-I stay here and die.

-You leave me no choice. Ramsay, begin your card reading. I was hoping that it could be different; but, I see that it can't.

Jeffrey hurried from the room and left myself, Mark, Lisa, and the dead man inside. I opened the box and drew out the five cards, but turning only one of them face-up.

THE PHYSICIAN

I knew what it meant and for this I hated Timothy and now wanted him dead.

-Forgive me, Ramsay.

-Forgiven.

-I am a coward.

Jeffrey came back into the room with his medical bag.

-You leave me no choice, Timothy. I cannot have priests in this sanctuary. This will be painless.

Jeffrey took out a hypodermic needle from his medical bag and approached Timothy. With an expert hand, he plunged the needle into his chest. In a matter of minutes, he was dead.

THE BLANK CARD

CHAPTER XIII
LISA

JEFFREY AND Mark carried out the body. Lisa and I were now alone in the drawing room.

-Ramsay, pour me a stiff drink, would you? I need one badly, rather.

I went to the sideboard and poured her straight Scotch. Lisa appeared to be crumbling in her chair.

-Are you all right?

-No. Not really. I'm next. I can't fake being brave anymore, can I? Even my sarcasm is beginning to wane.

-Here's your drink. How can anyone be brave?

-That's better. Nothing like good alcohol to stiffen the nerve. Well, darling, how long do I have and, please, don't be kind.

-A little less than a year; is that long enough?

-No. It will have to do, though, won't it?

I knelt down in front of her.

-Are you afraid to die, Lisa?

-I'm afraid of being bloody butchered, if that's what you mean. I do intend to enjoy the time that I have left, though. Poor Timothy...I don't know why he brooded for so long; but, I don't think of him as a coward. Do you?

-I'm sorry for what I said to him; but, how else could I feel? I seem to be the tool in all of this.

-Perhaps, I'll do myself in before my allotted time is up. I wonder what dear Jeffrey would say to that? Would it upset destiny's plans?

-I think my husband would understand.

-You don't sound too damned convincing. Why are you so hard on him? Still haven't forgiven him for murdering that cab driver in Egypt? Haven't you killed? I mean really, Ramsay, let go of it.

-Why should I?

-Because, it's nothing and there are far more important things to worry yourself about.

-Such as, Lisa?

-After Jeffrey's death, the game really begins. We'll find out if all the years of waiting were quite worth it. We'll find out if you're worth your salt, dear girl.

-What am I supposed to do?

-I'm sure you'll figure it out; you and our silent man, Mark.

-What do you know about Julietta?

-Me? Next to nothing. I've only spoken to her a few times, and never alone. I don't think she really likes me. I really don't care because I don't like her.

-What do you think of her?

-I've never really thought about her that much. I saw you watching her that other time.

-So did she.

The two of us laughed.

-Did you see how my husband fawned over her?

-Don't be too hard on the dear boy. Anyway, for a change, Julietta was giving out the information instead of taking it in; tossing hints about like bloody confetti.

-Who is she?

-I think she's not what she seems. And, I don't think Jeffrey is in love with her, if that's what has you worried. Not *in* love with her, if you get my gist.

-I don't.

-He dotes on her like a son would dote on his mother.

I sat back on my haunches, flabbergasted. Lisa smiled down slyly at me.

-That was very perceptive of you, Lisa. It would never have occurred to me.

-Well, you are a bit close to it.

-But, if Julietta is so old...how old must her son be?

-Does it really matter? He does perform adequately in bed, doesn't he?

-Quite well, in fact.

-Then?

-I suppose you're right; but, how old is he?

-God only knows. Julietta did mention Eve.

-That would be before the time of Sumer; that would be at least six thousand years ago! I don't believe it!

-You do. Maybe, she'll tell you her life's story someday. Now, that would be quite a tale.

Jeffrey came back into the room. Lisa excused herself and my husband and I sat there waiting...waiting...and listening to the sound of the rain...and the year was nearly up.

Lisa was in her apartment and I was at the small table with Jeffrey and Osiris sitting next to me.

THE PRIESTESS OF DECAY

Lisa had driven home to her place in the rain. Her frame of mind was not good. When she reached her apartment, she ran herself a bubble bath and then, quite calmly, she bathed.

-I've always rather fancied being butchered in a bubble bath; a bit like that Frenchman.

She took her time about it and, at first, didn't notice the lights dimming in the white tiled bathroom.

-Time to get out. I do believe I'm a coward.

She toweled herself dry and went, naked, to open the door.

-Damned dark in here. What's happened to the lights? I hope it's not a power outage.

Lisa opened the door and screamed. A priest was standing in the doorway. She slammed it shut, locked it and grabbed a large towel to drape about her body.

The small wall clock struck eight o'clock.

CAT AND MOUSE

A knife blade was thrust through the crack of the door. Lisa jumped back as the knife was forcing open the lock. The lights in the bathroom were almost completely off now.

PRIEST OF DEATH

-Can't even pick a bloody lock.

On impulse and nerve, Lisa opened the door and the priest fell inside. Nimbly, she stepped over him and made a dash for the front door. He came after her, but Lisa was too quick for him. She made it to the door and ran into the hallway screaming for help.

The stairwell was her only chance.

FUN AND GAMES

Lisa ran down the stairs at a frantic pace with the priest just a few steps behind her. She screamed and turned on him in mid-step. He couldn't stop himself in time and they both went crashing down the stairs. Lisa was the first to get up and, using the heel of her foot, she rammed it into his neck, breaking it.

-That was fun!

MAN OF DESTINY

Lisa made her way down to the main lobby and ran out into the street. Once on the corner, she signaled for a taxi, all the time laughing at herself and her frenzied appearance.

A car approached, but it wasn't a taxi. It stopped...and Lisa backed away. Its driver opened the door and beckoned her in. He took out his pistol and shot Lisa between the eyes. The impact of the bullet pushed her against the building and she slumped dead to the ground. Lisa had recognized her killer: Carmino.

THE BLANK CARD

CHAPTER XIV
JEFFREY

-INTERESTING.

-I thought this Carmino was on our side.

-He is. He at least made it painless for Lisa.

-And, you call that being on our side? I don't.

-Dear Ramsay, you must learn to trust me and to listen, truly listen, to what I tell you.

-Yes?

I was irritated by my own stubbornness.

-Carmino is a killer. He does what must be done. He has re-entered our lives and yours, in particular; beware of him!

-Jeffrey? I forgive you for what happened in Egypt those many years ago.

-Many years ago?

-To me, they seem like a lot of years. I don't want you to die.

Jeffrey sat down next to me and put out his cigarette in the ashtray by the small, wooden box.

-Thank you. That means a great deal to me.

-Lisa...we must go to her, Jeffrey.

-I've sent Mark to the police; his will be a new face and an unfamiliar name for them to speak with. I dare not go.

-Should I?

-Tell my fortune.

-No!

He lit another cigarette.

-I'll leave you now.

-Jeffrey, no!

I ran after him, but I was too slow. I saw his private office door close. Frantically, I ran to it and tried to open it. I started banging on it with my fists. But, what could happen? I wasn't reading the cards, so nothing could happen. Sounds came from within the office, and they were unpleasant sounds. This couldn't be happening!

-Jeffrey! Open the door. I won't read the cards! I'll burn them!

The sound of a body hitting the ground and a man's groan came to greet my ears. The body was being kicked about the floor. In a panic, I ran back to the drawing room for the cards. When I reached the door, I had to stop; a man was walking toward me. He was tall and slim with a gaunt face and a small, closely cropped goatee, but no moustache. He was bald, except for the sides of his head that held fine, short silvery hair. He was quite striking.

-Good evening.

He was playing with the cards, and I could see that he had dropped three of them to the floor.

-Don't do that! Are you insane?

I made to grab the cards from him, but he pulled back.

-Why not? He's the last to go so let's finish the game.

His voice was cynical and soft. His black, silk coat reached down to the floor.

-Who the hell are you? Give-me-those-cards!

Again, he backed away and dropped a fourth card to the floor.

-Just one more card, shall we?

-Who are you?

-Carmino.

I gasped.

-Takes your breath away, doesn't it? I knew it would.

I ran back to the office door.

-Too late, my sweet. He's as good as dead.

Turning about, I saw him drop a fifth card to the floor.

THE HANGED MAN

-The filth is now hoisting your near dead husband's body up to be hanged. By the way, he's been beaten to a pulp.

THE BLANK CARD

-I'll kill you for this!

I lunged for him, but he eluded me by simply walking backwards. How could that be? Carmino walked over to the fireplace and threw the deck of cards into the flames. Slowly, he picked up the five cards and tossed them in, as well.

-Done. I'll say goodbye for now. Don't bother to let me out.

He walked past me and left our house slamming the door behind him. I was alone now with my dead husband. None of the servants were in the house. A sharp knocking came to the door and I nearly jumped out of my skin.

-Who is it?

-Julietta. Open this door.

I flung it open; and her response, as usual, was unpredictable.

-I like you. You had enough wits about you to ascertain who was calling at such an ungodly time, and you didn't hesitate in letting me in.

She walked past me, stopped in front of Jeffrey's office and stared at the closed door.

-My son has been murdered and this sanctuary violated. Close and lock that door, at once. I must speak with you and our conversation must, of necessity, be brief and straight to the heart of the matter. Play time is over, and you are now alone, my dear.

-I still have Mark.

-You must not see him for a few years; many years it may seem to you, but the years will not be enough for the amount of work that you must do. You must learn and acquire even more knowledge than you presently possess. The edges must be smoothed out. Knowledge of the constellations and of astronomy- listen to what I say to you!

-I am.

-Go to the phone and call the police: say to them that burglars have broken in and killed your husband. This is no time to be weak; just do as I instruct you.

-I feel so disoriented.

-Phone the police, Ramsay. And, remember that you and Mark are now strangers to each other. It would be awkward for him to be associated with another murder.

-I understand.

-Be careful of what you say. The simple truth will suffice, with the proper omissions, of course.

The police were easy enough to handle; a smile and a pretty face rendered them into pliability. Perhaps, they had their suspicions...I didn't care. All alone was I to speak to them and to watch them carry out Jeffrey in the black bag. Before they arrived, though, Julietta did have a few other curious things to tell me.

-Are there any chocolates in the house?

-I'll get you some from the drawing room.

Julietta followed me in.

-Thank you. The estate will have to be settled, and the contents of the will may come as a shock to you. Jeffrey has left everything to me.

-What are you telling me?

I almost threw the chocolates in her face.

-He knew what his fate would be, and he wanted no suspicion to fall upon his wife. From you, he has removed any so-called motive of murder.

-I see...

-Now, calm yourself, and hand me the chocolates like a good girl. Of course, I will hand over everything to you, if you wish it. Or, I will act as your benefactress. I can be trusted, I assure you.

-I'll think about it.

-I would prefer an answer now.

-I trust you, Julietta.

-Good. Then, that is settled.

-When will I see Mark?

-In about twenty or twenty-five years...not so long a time, really. After Jeffrey's funeral, you must go into hiding. The priests may try to hunt you down and violate this sanctuary again. Carmino may try and reach you. Kill him, if you see him. He enjoyed orchestrating my son's death.

-He enjoyed it. I saw that.

-I will make him pay for that.

Julietta popped another chocolate into her mouth. How man had she eaten?

-From time to time, you may stop here and see to the upkeep of the place. I know you'll miss it.

-What about Jeffrey's body?

-The police will entrust it to his wife, of course. I will come back for the funeral and see to the interment of the body. I must go. I will see to your travel arrangements, for you mustn't remain here long.

I walked with her to the door and we kissed each other goodbye. Her skin was soft and smooth, but there was a coldness to it.

I watched her walk to the waiting car. In another moment, she drove off.

Closing the door behind me, I walked toward Jeffrey's office. I dared not go in and disturb anything. Twenty years of marriage were over. I walked back to the drawing room and waited for the police to arrive.

Fear.

Isolation.

But, not despair. And, of course, I didn't cry.

My sister, Maria, looked at me as I made ready to go to bed. After thirty years of virtual solitude, I still had work to do...work that I did not want to do.

BOOK IV
MARK

CHAPTER XV
THE GYMNASIUM

YOU'VE HEARD Ramsay speak about me and now it's my time to tell my own story. Naked, I walked across the wooden floor that I had polished the other day and headed for the bathroom. Osiris, Jeffrey's cat, followed me. He's over fifty years old and still he retains his youthfulness. I loved this cat, and Jeffrey left him in my care.

I turned to the mirror to face myself. Sunlight poured through the window. My body is still young and firm and I'm every bit the athlete that I always was. The body is smooth and chiseled and the uncut manhood can still get an erection to satisfy any woman or man. I've allowed my face to age to a degree: the lines and slight weathering have set in, but there is a beauty to that.

The work that lies ahead is difficult and, perhaps, impossible. Jeffrey said it could be done and that it had been done at different points in antiquity. I'll share with you our objective: Ramsay and I must raise from the dead our eight comrades, and we haven't much time to do it.

I closed the shower taps and step out of the stall glistening wet and dripping all over the damned floor. I look to see if Osiris is still in the room. He is and he's staring up at me, wide- eyed and filled with curiosity. With a towel flung over my shoulder, I walked out of the bathroom and crossed the hall into my bedroom. Osiris followed me in.

If I don't hurry, I'll be late and I don't want to keep Ramsay waiting. But, I can't seem to push myself into putting any clothes on.

What should I tell you about myself: everything or nothing? The beginnings of my life aren't important. They're filled with pain and despair and loneliness...a loneliness which still has not been lifted. Allyson couldn't lift it nor could Jeffrey.

I ran my hand through my short, blonde and grey hair and, then, placed that hand on my erection, trying to calm it into flaccidity. My hands...lined with tiny scars from my ritual accident, which was not an accident for no accident could have had so much cunning behind it. There is a traitor in our group who will have to be brought back to life with the others.

The solar flame is still rising in the morning sky and the golden sunlight is filtering through the blinds. Osiris pounces on the solar lines and plays in them.

Allyson and Jeffrey, the two people whom I love the most, are dead. I mourn for then still. I wonder if Ramsay mourns Jeffrey's death? Somehow, I don't think that she does. Their marriage was complex and not a happy one.

I'll tell you my brief story while I get dressed.

My life began at fifteen when I met Jeffrey Bast. I was working out in the gymnasium on the lower west side of Manhattan. It was a sparse and hygienic place which specialized in free-weights. How well I remember that day. It was early spring and the wind still had a bracing chill to it. The sun was golden and there wasn't a cloud in the sky. Like a fool, I was sunbathing on the roof having just taken an ice cold shower. The elements don't bother me so long as there is sunlight to reach my body and my eyes.

I was lying on one of the wooden chairs wearing my white gym shorts. I was trying to think about how I had had to leave school and find work that would bring some money to me and my mother. Working at the gymnasium seemed ideal to me: the pay was crummy, but the benefits were good: free work-out time and a free lunch of cold sandwiches every day. I worked hard and long hours for my pay and privileges and now it was lunch time and I wanted to relax from the cleaning up and the washing of towels and shower floors and steam rooms and working the front desk.

The roof door opened and a shadow crossed over me. The darkness of that shadow was penetrating and a little frightening. I opened my eyes and saw a tall, handsome man standing next to me. I stared up at him.

-Hello, young man. May I sit down next to you? I won't be intrusive.

-I don't mind.

-Thank you.

Like me, he was wearing gym shorts. He rested his lean body next to mine.

-It's brisk and cold today, but the sun is shining. What's your name?

-Marcus.

-Marcus, my name is Jeffrey Bast. You may call me Jeffrey. It's good that we're alone up here. It will give us a chance to talk. I know that you work here, because I have observed you and how you carry yourself.

-I haven't seen you around before.

-I know that you haven't. You didn't see me because it wasn't yet time for you to see me.

-What do you want from me?

-Everything. And, in return, you will have everything. Shall I continue, Marcus?

-I guess I don't have anything to lose. Call me Mark.

-You're wrong. You will lose a miserable and poor life of self-degradation; do you understand that? You will be uplifted from the rabble and your eyes will be opened toward the stars. You are now a fallen god, as I am, and others like us; but, you will, once again, in a moment of millennia untold, be placed upon your throne of light.

He paused for just a moment.

-Your mother will be provided for until she dies. A life of worry and strain and any emotional bond will be lifted from your shoulders and your mind. All you need to give in return is everything. Do you agree to this?

-Why me? Who am I to rate all of this?

-You are who you were. I will be your mentor and you will be my student. Say that you agree and we'll leave this gymnasium together.

I agreed.

CHAPTER XVI
THE MASTERS

I CARRIED a black, duffel bag and in it were magical weapons: a dagger, a silver chain, and also a pair of ice skates. Allyson taught me how to skate, and I still enjoy the sport tremendously. I'll take a cab into the city, and tell you of other things that should be told to you. A cab waited on the corner because I willed-it-to-be-there. A magician manipulates his environment through his mind.

When I first arrived at Jeffrey's house, I felt acutely my humble beginnings. But, when he spoke to me, he put me completely at my ease, assuming that I knew nothing in this lifetime.

First, I had to learn all the basics of gracious living: table manners and proper English and how to dress and carry myself with dignity and discretion. I had no need to support myself. Jeffrey had a knowledge of the underpinnings of money and gold, that precious metal which turns this globe upon its axis. He was also a gambler and a good one, often ruining the lives of other men; but, such was their own willful intention and rotten luck.

I soon met his friends and associates who seemed to take to me as if I had never been a stranger and for this I was suitably grateful. Allyson I loved at once. I loved her for her beauty and charm and her refreshing shyness and reserve. Like myself, she had been transformed into the beautiful swan by the sculptor's hand. On the ice, her artistry was unsurpassed and, although, her athletic abilities were good, her technique was not good enough to earn her many gold medals. So what?

And, of course, I was versed in the occult arts every day and almost every moment. This was difficult for me because memorization has never been my strength, but determination has made up for that deficiency. Tutored in ancient and ceremonial magic, my time was never spent in boredom or apprehension of the future. The future beyond the future was soon to be arrived at.

There is one incident that I should relate to you; and it's the only time when I spied on Jeffrey. Anyway, I think that he knew.

It must have been early morning. I couldn't sleep and, for some reason, Osiris kept pawing at my forehead. He wanted me to get up and out of bed and follow him. I did just that because I always obey that cat.

Naked, I got up and left my room to follow Osiris down the dark corridor. Down the corridor and up a staircase, I followed the quick, small cat. On the next floor, there were, at intervals, light globes hanging from the ceiling which cast eerie and distorted shadows that gave one the impression of being underwater.

Osiris stopped just at the end of the corridor in front of a door and beckoned me to open it. It was a temple room and almost entirely bare of any furnishings. There was a curtain of many colors to the far side and, silently, I approached this beautiful thing. I heard voices... strange and frightening voices; but one voice was familiar.

-Ramsay is to be brought into the group. Time is now an enemy. On the night that you meet her, you will marry her and take her to the wedding chamber. Then, you must proceed without hesitation. The collapse will soon occur.

-Yes.

-What more do you have to say to us?

-The future of futures depends on Ramsay.

-As ordained.

The curtain billowed and I thought they were about to come out. It was Osiris. I scooped him up; but, I didn't leave. I wanted to hear more.

-Our enemies lurk everywhere.

-They will not dare strike until Ramsay heralds that hour. Even in this lifetime, she has command over her enemies. She is a formidable opponent and ally.

-Will her loyalty prove as strong?

-It will.

I slipped away, carrying Osiris in my arms. On that night, I had heard the voices of Jeffrey's masters.

CHAPTER XVII
"THE ACCIDENT"

ONE NIGHT, about a year before Ramsay arrived, I laid in bed wearing only my ritual robe and with my prayer book at my side. I'd done no preparation that day for our forthcoming ritual, and that was much out of character for I would often go into the chamber hall and at least "run through" the ritual. On that day, neither Osiris nor I emerged from our room.

It was only with the evening hour that I emerged to take the ritual bath. I went with Jeffrey to one bathroom and Kenjiro, Timothy, and Armando went to another, larger bathroom. Jeffrey ran the tap water for me and added salt to cleanse and unite with the body.

I stripped down and shut off the bronze taps and climbed into the tub. I immersed myself in the bathwater and put my head under the water to ease my senses. No soap is used in the ritual bath because of the dread of impurities that are contained within them. I lounged there for a few moments wanting my body to soak in the sacred fluids. Jeffrey glanced over at me and smiled.

-Is my beautiful boy enjoying his bath?

-Yes. Thank you. But, I have to get out and prepare your bath. May I?

-Please. Dry yourself off thoroughly.

He smiled with benevolence and beauty. I got out of the tub and dried my body; then, I drained and washed the bathtub. Jeffrey had stripped naked and walked over to me. Gently, he placed his hand on my shoulder.

-I love you.

-I love you.

-Always stay with me, my beautiful boy. One day, Mark, I must ask you to help me and our friends to rise from our graves and to reverse the cycle of death. You will do that for me?

-I will.

-Swear it.

-I swear it.

-May I hold you close to me, Mark, as I once did long ago in an ancient city called Pompeii? We were lovers, then.

We held each other close to the heart. I could feel his heart beating and his hands held my back with strength and conviction. Each of us grew hard as men do, but it was not this kind of love which held us: it was our pure, platonic love for each other. We kissed and his breath tasted sweet and cold. He began to stroke the back of my head and, then, I knew it was time to lead him to his ritual bath. I would bathe my Master. He stepped into the tub, and I applied the sponge to every part of his smooth, alabaster skin taking special care with the most precious part of a man.

-Are you ready, Mark?

-Just about. You look handsome in your robe.

-Let's go.

Jeffrey switched off the lights, and I followed him into the dark hallway. We were two solemn figures walking down the corridor in our bare feet and white, cotton kaftans that Allyson had sewn for us: my beautiful Allyson.

In a few moments, we met the other members of our encampment who were waiting for us outside the chamber room. We nodded to them in greeting as I gazed at Allyson for just a moment. She caught my glance and smiled. Jeffrey proceeded on into the chamber room with Tana, who closed the door. The rest of us waited outside as the priest and priestess readied the chamber room for the mass.

None of us spoke, but Armando looked restless. He had been standing next to Tana when Jeffrey and I had arrived. Timothy stood in silence at the threshold to the ritual chamber. Among us all, he alone was dressed in black: dangling from his waist was a sword with which he would have no compunction in using on any trespasser.

The door opened and Tana came out to beckon us into the temple chamber. We obeyed, and she withdrew into the corridor to await being called upon by the deacon, Kenjiro.

Once inside the chamber, we took our places on small cushions that had been set up for us. Only a few small candles lit the room with incense permeating the air.

Kenjiro began the Mass in a low and somber voice as he placed the barriers of protection around us. Soon, the priestess would be allowed to enter the chamber. Kenjiro would open the portal for her. The deacon finished a silent prayer of supplication. The prayer book was in front of him, but he didn't read from it. His prayer was well memorized.

The time came for the priestess to enter. Kenjiro walked to the door and pulled the barrier open. Tana was waiting outside dressed in a blue, filmy robe...and her look was one of seduction. Kenjiro stepped aside and allowed her to cross the sacred threshold of the unseen things of wisdom. When Tana entered, she looked at me with contempt. What had I done to deserve such a look of contempt? I have my suspicions.

The priest left his confinement to join his priestess who now stood before him with outstretched arms. And...there are parts of the Mass which mustn't be spoken of, not even in the waning days of this known reality. The priest made the circuit of the temple and, then, knelt before the altar in front of the now seated priestess. The prayers were said and the responses were given. There now came that time during the Mass when my vision blurred and I could barely read the printed word so ionized had the air become and so charged with forces that govern our seen phenomena.

We were now permitted to stand and receive the consecrated wine. As I prepared to receive the wine, I noticed that the lamp was burning brighter than it should have been: the lamp which hung just above the altar to light the way.

Tana was ready to pour the wine. The lamp was directly above my head and Allyson stood to my left waiting to receive the wine. I felt an intense heat above me; perspiration broke out on my forehead. Jeffrey sensed what was about to happen, but too late. The oil lamp burst into flame and rained down upon me. Allyson would have also been injured, but I pushed her violently back to safety. My body was consumed in an oily flame which crept along my body like a living, venomous substance.

Jeffrey flung the wine bottle aside and came to help me survive this horror. He ripped off his robe and threw it over my writhing form. I was screaming in agony. Allyson ran over to help him and between the two of them, they covered me in the soft kaftan...still the searing, orange flames moved across my body...my face...my face!

Tana jumped off the altar and began screaming like a madwoman. Timothy ran over to her and slapped her hard across the face several times. Armando laughed at that as Lisa was trying to put out the lamp which was still in flames and threatening to burn the house down. Lisa yelled over to Armando to come over and help her. He did, but still he laughed.

Timothy was now helping Jeffrey and Allyson who threw themselves on top of me to smother the flames. At last the flames had gone out. Kenjiro ran out of the temple to fetch his healing oils which would save my face and my body...with time and long suffering.

Allyson could now begin to cry.

Gently, Jeffrey picked me up and carried me to his medical room downstairs. Allyson followed him while the others remained to clean things up in the temple room; the place was a shambles. When we reached the main corridor, Jeffrey let Allyson move ahead to open the several doors that led to his office. Only a few dimly lit bulbs showed the way, but Allyson knew her way and didn't hesitate.

At last, I was placed on the cold, metal table. I screamed in pain as my friends stripped me of what was left of my burnt and shredded robe. Allyson put her hands to her mouth to stifle a scream as Jeffrey turned on the overhead lights. Kenjiro hurried in with a jar containing a hazy fluid: the oils which he constantly swore by. Well, Kenjiro, old friend, they would now be put to the test. Jeffrey looked concerned about using them.

-Jeffrey, let him. It will work! I know it will.

-Very well, Allyson . Heal my son, Kenjiro.

-Hold the boy down and have the bandages ready to place on his skin. Both of you will be needed. Allyson, lock that door, please. None of those others must interrupt with their senseless questions.

The door was locked and Kenjiro began to apply the oil. He dipped his hands into the glass jar and spread copious amounts all over my body while Jeffrey and Allyson gently bandaged every limb and surface. Allyson never stopped crying.

Kenjiro applied the healing oil to my face with loving delicacy.

-I will bandage the boy's face myself

Jeffrey cut him enough length of gauze and the Asian man did a masterful job. The work was now complete. I lay there on the table motionless and bandaged. My feet had been spared the conflagration, so I would have movement. My vision was greatly impaired but, in time, it would restore itself, for the most part. So masterfully had my friends bandaged me that I was able to actually move and flex my arms and legs, albeit with a great deal of pain. Slowly, I raised myself from the table. Allyson made to help me, but the two men held her back.

-Let the boy move on his own power.

I did so for the next eleven years. My face would heal and my hair would grow back... slowly. However, some scars were too deep to heal.

Ramsay was fascinated by the bandaged man whom she first saw at our dinner table on the night she came to marry Jeffrey. And, today, she will be my fellow life-giver. But, would she be willing? I fear not.

CHAPTER XVIII
THE CAFE

RAMSAY WAS waiting for me in front of the skating pavilion. She was wearing sun glasses and a dark hat. She waved to me.

-Mark, my darling!

I kissed her, but held back any kind of passion.

-You may kiss me, again, if you wish.

-No.

Ramsay ignored my curt answer.

-I know of a secluded café that I want to show you. We can sit there and order coffees and cakes and talk undisturbed for as long as we want. Do you want that, Mark?

-Look, clouds are gathering on the horizon.

-They give me comfort. Let's hurry, darling.

We walked down a number of streets and, only occasionally, did she take her glance from me.

-I love you.

-In my own way, Ramsay, I love you, as well. Are we almost at your café? I feel exposed in the city.

-Yes. But, it's not really a café; nothing as open or public as that. It's within the plaza's complex and it's underground. They have all flavors of coffees there and delicious cakes and pastries.

-I'm hungry.

-I've been hungry for a long time, also. Let's hurry, then.

She took me to her underground restaurant, and ordered coffees and cakes for us; and, like a lovely girl, she brought them to the table and sat down next to me.

-Taste your coffee, darling, and tell me that it tastes wonderful.

-It does; but, it needs to cool off a bit.

-And, now, your cake...a big, healthy bite. Go on.

-Delicious. Thank you for taking me here.

-Eat and drink more. Feast!

I did. And, now we had to talk in this large, but fairly deserted place. The lighting was low and the background music was pleasant.

-Ramsay?

-Yes?

-We have a lot to do. The road before us is a pretty difficult one. Time is running out for everything.

-I know this. Go on, I'm listening.

-The dead must be raised from their graves and the chord of life must be re-attached.

-How?

-Together, we have to go back to that place where Jeffrey took you on your honeymoon: the ruined temple near Memphis. Do you know the way?

-I- I think so. That's a long time ago, Mark. It's nearly fifty years ago! I think I can find it.

-But?

-Why must we do this?

-Ramsay?

-Mark, they're dead.

-Yes?

-Don't look at me that way. I loved Jeffrey, but to raise a thing from its grave...is it right? Does anyone have the right, Mark, to play God?

-Perhaps, one day, we'll be as gods. Maybe, this is practice time for us.

-Don't joke about it. I know what has to be done, but why must it be done?

-After the end, Ramsay, there will be another beginning and a new hierarchy that we'll be a part of: a hierarchy that others will want to take away from us.

-The priests?

-The murdering pigs who call themselves priests.

-So twelve of us form a new hierarchy: a new dynasty of gods, is that it?

-Yes. We have to make our plans for departure and we must do it quickly.

-That can be done today. I can be ready by this evening, is that fast enough for you?

-Don't be annoyed with me. I didn't mean to be harsh with you just now, but our lives are in constant danger. We should no longer be separated.

-On that, I agree with you, darling. But-

-What is it?

-I just felt someone walk over my grave. I think I may be catching a cold; put your arm about me.

-Here, drink your coffee, Ramsay, it's still hot.

-There's someone here with us who shouldn't be here.

The two of us looked around the restaurant.

-A priest is here.

-Let's stay put and wait the bastard out. I'll get more coffee.

-No! Don't leave my side.

-I'll be right back.

-Hurry!

I got up to get the coffees and to have a closer look at the patrons. My eyes found their target: a priest. He was sitting over to one side and avoiding my glance. His top hat and overcoat were not concealment enough: a filthy haze hovered about him. Ramsay and I had to act.

I walked back to our table and the look on my face conveyed what I'd just seen. Ramsay's response was interesting. I saw the rage building up within her.

-A priest is here, Ramsay.

-Now what?

-I'll kill him.

-Do that, Mark. It'll be one less for us to worry about.

-They almost never travel alone these pigs. It'll serve as an example to the rest of them that we're not to be taken lightly.

-And, what about us?

-The adventure begins.

-I don't want it to begin. I'll settle for a few years with you and, then, we can walk into oblivion together. I won't care.

-Won't you?

-I don't think I will very much.

-I will.

-Mark, they're dead. Let them stay dead.

-A new civilization is depending on us. We have no choice in this, Ramsay: none of us has a choice against destiny. Our fate is still in our own hands and, yet it's still in another's.

-Whose?

-Our superiors.

-Mark, you're talking in riddles.

-We love each other.

-Yes!

-Now, your love for me must take you with me. I can't do it alone, but if you force my hand, I'll attempt it. Are you prepared to accept the consequences for that?

-No. I can't accept that.

-I'm glad to hear that. Now, let's go to the bastard's table. I have my knife with me.

There were no more words spoken between us as we walked the short distance to the priest.

-You.

It was the only word I spoke to the priest before plunging the knife into his throat. Ramsay had her back to us and managed to conceal the deed from the other patrons. The priest was unable to cry out or even gasp. The horror on his face was satisfying.

I grabbed Ramsay by the sleeve and led her out of the restaurant. The priest slid off the chair and, then, the pandemonium began. We walked rapidly down the passage and up the flight of stairs.

-My car is parked only a few blocks away. You drive, Mark.

She flung the keys at me, and we continued walking at a good clip. Tonight, we would have to leave the country.

-Darling, why are we driving out of the city? Let's go to my town house, everything that we could possibly want is there.

-We will but, first, I have to drive home and pick up my passport.

-Oh! Mark, I'm sorry.

-And, pack a suitcase and pick up Osiris. Then, we can go to your town house.

-Is it wise to come back into the city?

-I'm not too concerned about the police. I don't think we have to worry about them too much because there'll be no body in the restaurant when they get there. Our friends can't afford to be discovered or hampered by the likes of the cops. They'll have to cover their track and adjust to their losses..

-So, if there's no body...

-We have nothing to fear. But, I don't want to take a chance of being delayed. The cops might ask some awkward questions that we'd have a tough time answering.

Within the hour, we were back in Manhattan.

-Hey, Ramsay, Osiris likes being in his master's house, again; look at him scampering about.

-Good for him. It's always disturbed me to have Jeffrey and the others so close; especially my husband. I expect him to rise from his coffin every night.

-He will and very soon. Does that scare you?

-Mark, do you even have to ask?

-I shouldn't have. Sorry.

-I just need to check the windows and make sure the servants have their orders clear.

-We have time. I'll put your things in the hallway.

Ramsay was gone for just a few minutes.

-I'm ready.

-Let's go.

CHAPTER XIX
EGYPT, AGAIN

THE PLANE was jolted and Ramsay held on to my arm. Everyone aboard was sleeping now except for the crew members and the two of us. The cabin was dimly lit and it felt almost cozy. Ramsay drank her second cup of coffee.

-Is that how you stay so thin?

-Why through magic, of course, Mark.

-Of course.

-Mark?

-Yes?

-Your voice sounds so harsh. Why don't the priests kill us? Why have they waited so long?

-I think they're waiting for us to succeed.

-Do I dare ask why?

-To learn the secrets of life and death and, then, to slaughter us.

-But, they're the ancient priests, don't they know all of this?

-Not all of it. Interesting how you hit upon the truth in your questions.

-What about Julietta and Carmino?

-What about those two characters? They're of no use to us- well, maybe, Julietta is; but, we can't count on her for anything in the way of practical help.

-And, Carmino?

-I'm sure that Julietta would like to kill him. He's really not completely bad; but, I wouldn't turn my back on him.

-Where are they hiding all the time?

-Look out the window, Ramsay, see the darkness.

-Yes...

-There and nowhere and, frankly, I don't give a crap where they are. Carmino was in on Lisa's and Jeffrey's death. He plays both sides of the fence and I'd like to shove him off his perch.

-Do you want to kill him?

-No. I'd like to make him subservient to me and clip his wings a little.

-Don't say that, Mark.

-Why not? Disappointed in me?

-Surprised.

-Shocked?

-No. Just a little surprised.

-Maybe, you thought I was above something like that? Carmino is one of us, and I don't kill my own kind. I would teach him some badly needed lessons, though.

Ramsay stared into her now empty coffee cup.

-Still not satisfied with my answer?

-I only met Carmino once and my own impulse was to kill him.

-Were you attracted to him? He can be a pretty charming guy.

-Yes.

-I like your honesty, Ramsay? Why?

-I found his appearance striking...unusual. He reminded me of a French dissident for some reason.

-Did he now?

-Are you jealous?

-Not particularly.

-Bastard. I want you to be jealous.

-I know. What's your impression of the enigmatic Julietta?

-She reminds me of a mannequin.

-Perceptive.

-Is she a mannequin?

-You'll have to ask her.

-You're laughing at me.

-If you knew the truth about her, you'd laugh, too.

-Tell me the truth.

-Your husband will when he awakens.

Ramsay turned away from me to look out the window.

-We'll be landing soon.

-What of it?

-Look at me, Ramsay.

-Leave me alone. I think I hate you all and myself, the most.

-There are priests on this plane.

-Tell me something I don't know.

-Do you know that they mean to kill us?

She turned to look at me.

-I thought they needed us. You said so.

-They probably want to take us as prisoners.

-No one will take me prisoner.

-Keep your voice down. As soon as the plane lands, we have to be the first ones off; everything depends on that. We mustn't draw attention to ourselves in Egypt. We have to go quietly about our mission and leave just as inconspicuously. We have only carry-ons with us and that'll save time. Get your bag from the overhead compartment. The plane's starting to descend.

-Again, I'll be seeing Egypt in darkness as I did fifty years ago. Is there no end to the darkness? I'm sick of it. I thought you would change that for me, Mark.

-It will change, but not because of me. Don't give me too much credit.

-That's pretty disappointing, you know.

-Do you have everything?

-I love you, Mark.

-Are you ready?

-Another disappointment.

As soon as the plane door opened, Ramsay and I made our way toward the hatchway. I had my one suitcase and Ramsay had hers. We each carried concealed knives. Customs went smoothly and, then, Ramsay rented us a car.

-Ramsay, you're driving too fast.

-Yes?

-I guess we'll get there faster.

-What happens when we get there, Mark? Do I go down into the temple vaults and follow my instincts? I really don't know.

-We have to take one particular scroll, an ankh, a scarab, and a small tube fashioned of gold; it's part of Jeffrey's inheritance. We won't be stealing anything, if that's what's worrying you.

-Oh? Try telling all that to the Egyptian police. How do you propose to smuggle these souvenirs out of the country?

-How else is it done?

-By bribing the right people.

-Good girl.

-I think we're almost there.

-You remember your last visit?

-Some of it, not much.

The wind began to pick up. Ramsay switched on the windshield wipers.

-And, another thing, Mark, you led me to believe the priests would make an attempt to kill us back at the airport. They didn't. You want to explain that one?

-They've been following us.

-How very boring! I'm bored with them and their little cat and mouse games. If only I could kill them all and be done with this. Maybe, I'll let them catch up to us...what would you say to that?

-You just might get your wish. How would you kill them?

-A thrust of the knife will do nicely. To see their blood spilling into the sand...blood and sand...wasn't that the name of a movie?

We laughed for a moment.

-Look! I think I can see the ruins. Do you see them, Mark?

-Yes. Slow down.

She stopped the car just short of the temple's perimeter.

-Mark?

-Let's go.

As we stepped out of the car, the sand and wind pushed against us from every direction. We could barely keep our eyes open and our breathing came in short, painful gasps.

-Take my hand.

-It's worse than before.

-That's always the case. I think I can hear another car in the distance.

-I can't.

-Trust me. It's probably our friends.

-Now, I hear it. Mark, you were right.

In another moment, we were standing in the middle of the temple amidst the megalithic stones which predated ancient Egypt. I stood behind Ramsay and placed my hands over her eyes and gently applied pressure.

She would now have to make the journey alone into the tunnels below. I would stay above to protect her physical body.

Ramsay's etheric form descended into the subterranean temple. Her ancient memories would now come back to her. Her etheric body would be safe from all the deadly traps set by the priests so long ago; an astral descent was the only way it could be done. The priests were in the corridor with her...following Ramsay's ethereal image. They were powerless to stop her, but they could observe her.

And, now the narrative is no longer mine to tell. I have to let another do that job for me: the scribe.

BOOK V
RESURRECTION

CHAPTER XX
ANCIENT SOUVENIRS

THE CAR parked next to Ramsay's vehicle just outside the perimeter of the temple's holy circle. A figure emerged and came towards Mark.

-Good evening, Marcus.

It had been a long time since he'd been called by his proper name. Ramsay felt Mark's wavering attention.

-What is he doing up there? Does he want to place me in even more danger?

At that moment, Ramsay saw the sacred objects that she'd come for. Could her ethereal form grasp them? She found the answer to that puzzle as she placed her hand upon the ankh. Ramsay "lifted" the astral essence of that precious object. The priests watched her. Ramsay's hand went to the holy scarab and that sacred object's essence was "lifted"...its spiritual double.

-So far, it's gone well.

Mark picked up that thought as did Julietta.

-My son's wife is a gifted young woman. But, the job isn't completed, is it Marcus?

-Not yet.

-You don't ask me why I am here. Why is that? Could you be so displeased?

-My attention needs to be focused at the moment.

-Of course. Perhaps, I should remain silent? You look handsome, as always.

-You're beautiful, as always.

-Yes! As always...always! And, still, I must go on. Pity me, but not too heavily.

Ramsay's hand now touched the papyrus and extracted its essence. Her old skills as a priestess and magician were guiding her. Only one more sacred object to go...the most deadly and precious of all: the gold cylinder of life and death. It was behind the veil of Isis. It had to be there; but Ramsay was afraid to set foot in that sacred area.

-She hesitates.

Julietta offered Mark a piece of chocolate.

-No. Thank you.

-I'll have to eat the entire bar myself. I shall.

She unwrapped the foil and broke off a small piece.

-Still my daughter-in-law hesitates. Why? Urge her on Marcus; tell her not to fear and get her back here in one piece, of course.

Ramsay walked toward the veil. She passed its perimeter and found herself in an almost empty room. The gold cylinder was placed on the lap of Isis.

-Dare I touch it?

Julietta grew impatient.

-Foolish to have come so far and to stop now. Foolish.

Ramsay touched the gold cylinder.

-Excellent! Marcus, bring her back and watch the miracle of magical workings. Ramsay has done well and now you must complete your part. Do it!

Ramsay came back to her physical body with a start. Julietta was facing her and she took the sacred objects from her hands.

-I must kiss my daughter-in-law. We have done what few others have dared. And, now for the most dreadful task of all: to raise the dead from their graves!

CHAPTER XXI
CARMINO

THE WEATHER in New York was dreadful: bleak and pouring rain with little difference between day and night. The three occultists felt isolated from the world. The town house was their only anchor to the physical world and that same refuge seemed to be under attack by the elements. It was impossible to see the outside world from any window in the house because every transparent barrier was covered with mist. The inside of the house was warm, yet there were chilly spots to be found...eight of them. The three people inside carefully avoided these spots.

Mark emerged from the ritual bath covered in a white robe. Ramsay was waiting for him.

-I wanted to fetch your slippers for you, but I couldn't find them.

-I never wear any. I prefer the feel of the ground on my bare feet.

-Will you get dressed now? Julietta is waiting for us. She says that we don't need ceremonial robes. However, she advises us to wear black. The dead will see them and know that we're their friends.

-Yes?

-Mark, I'm frightened. What will happen tonight? Will they be as they were or different, somehow? Listen to that terrible rain and thunder, my love. Let's stop this madness and simply be together with each other. I'm begging you, Mark! Don't force my hand into participation tonight. Hold me!

Mark held her, but there was no affection or love. Ramsay withdrew from him and leaned against the wall.

-How bitter that was. You could have at least pretended.

Lightning struck the antennae of the roof and the two of them started.

-It should have struck me instead. No. Don't touch me. Soon, I will have a husband, again.

Ramsay walked away from the man she had loved for over half a century. Her emotions had to be readjusted and her feelings transferred to another. She descended the stairs of the dark house, listening to the rain and seeing nothing in particular. She was still wearing her street clothes: a black outfit that she had picked up in Paris a long time ago. Jeffrey would see her as she wanted to be seen, and he will approve. Ramsay was re-lieved that this thought brought a smile to her face. Her focus was shifting and the direction it was taking was for her own well-being.

Where was Julietta?

A knock at the door nearly caused her to slip on the final step of the staircase.

-Who is there?

-Carmino. You know me.

Ramsay unbolted the door and flung it open. A man stood before her who was dressed in black. His black rain coat was glistening with moisture and the black fe-dora concealed a part of his face.

-Come in, Carmino.

-Thank you.

Carmino placed his umbrella in the stand by the door and took off his rain coat and hat. He wore a black suit with a matching black shirt. As Ramsay placed his hat on the table, she couldn't help but stare at him. It made no difference to Carmino because he enjoyed be-ing stared at, especially by a beautiful woman. He strolled into the hallway and sat on the high oak table to take a good look at his hostess. He nodded approvingly at what he saw. Ramsay smiled for she also enjoyed be-ing stared at.

-May I offer you anything?

-You may offer me many things, Ramsay; but, at the moment, a cigarette is needed. Fetch me one, please?

Ramsay smiled over her shoulder at him as he got off the table and followed her into the historic drawing room.

-On the end table, Carmino, help yourself.

-And, a straight scotch and don't ruin it.

-What brings you here?

She brought over his drink. Carmino crossed his legs and nodded his thanks.

-I've come here to rejoin this group. Do you hear that rain? I find in it a soothing quality...a protection.

-I don't.

Ramsay sat down next to him on the couch and crossed her legs. Carmino appreciated this gesture and this woman.

-You asked me a direct question, Ramsay. Ask me another.

-When you put it like that, I can't think of anything to say.

-Then, I'll ask you a question to keep the conversation going.

-Please. I'll try not to be a bore.

-Have you been told all the salient facts; and, if you have, do you accept them?

-I'm a little hazy on some points, so my so-called acceptance is impossible. Would you be willing to smooth out the edges for me?

-I'm a direct man, however untrustworthy you may think me. Don't protest. We've no time to waste on civilities. Monumental tasks await us and I'm not certain of my welcome here.

-I welcome you here. I'm the mistress of this house.

Carmino took a drag on his cigarette.

-The end of the known universe is almost upon us. Everything will contract: fold up into a small ball, so to speak, and be consumed into the abyss.

-The abyss?

-A scientist would most likely call it a black hole: a collapsor. The physical universe is doomed, Ramsay, but we are to survive into the next epic incarnation as the new class of gods: the new dynasty.

-You'll have to explain that one.

-Most scientists are fools. They've failed to combine astronomy with the much older science of astrology. They know not of whence they theorize. The universe which we find ourselves occupying now is within the confines of a black hole. The collapse that will occur will push us through, literally, into the true universe of the cause...God's universe, shall we say?

-And, how are we supposed to survive this collapse? Can anything survive it?

Lightning flashed outside and, for a moment, the room was illuminated. The effect made Ramsay start, but it had no effect on her guest.

-We will. However, we must resurrect the others first and, in particular, your husband. He must signal the gods for the solar boat so that we may climb into it and be protected. It will point us directly into our sun, and we will pierce the outer veil and be borne through its center into the new universe.

-Everyone and everything else will die?

-Not precisely. The physical essence will be combined into the unity of a pure energy: all matter will return to its primeval essence: other dimensions, however, will survive.

-The vibrational essence.

-Yes. The vibratory core of each soul and of each planet and star will survive in its pure form ready to once again incarnate in the new universe. Nothing ever dies.

-I need a cigarette. It's all clear to me, now, but no less frightening. Our own sun is at the very center of the universe and everything will collapse into it. So, Carmino, why have we been chosen and what part do those priests play in all of this?

-Most of us have incarnated many times and our experience and growth have proclaimed us as heirs to the present gods, who themselves will evolve into higher states of consciousness. Your many incarnations, Ramsay, have paid your price of passage.

-You said that "most" of us have incarnated many times; what did you mean by that?

-You're sharp. Julietta and I have never died: within the same bodies we have remained for thousands of years.

-What are you telling me?

-Julietta and Jeffrey should tell you their own stories.

-Tell me yours.

-I'm a world traveler and that's all I'll tell you.

-The priests?

-Pieces of garbage who seek to gain entrance to the solar boat; one or two of them may succeed.

-Why? How?

Carmino edged closer to his hostess and their thighs touched.

-There is a traitor within this group, and that traitor must be found out and eliminated.

-And, be replaced by a priest?

-Balance must be struck and maintained: better a known quantity than a traitor.

-That does make sense, but-

-Yes?

-Can we trust you, Carmino?

-Only to a very fine point.

-Are you here now to save your own neck or to help us?

-You've answered your own question. Jeffrey married well.

He took another cigarette from the tray and Ramsay lit it for him.

-So, the priests are waiting outside to butcher us.

-Yes. They want us to raise our dead in order to show them how it's done.

-So, they can raise their dead, the few that we've managed to kill off?

-Yes.

Ramsay switched off the light nearest to her. Suddenly, she feared the light's exposure.

-You may place your arm about my shoulder, Carmino.

-It took you long enough. And, may I also do this?

He kissed her hard and proper. Ramsay was responsive. She transferred her hatred of Mark to a sexual passion for this intriguing man.

-You do that very well. Let me close the door.

Ramsay bolted the door and ran back to Carmino, who was now standing up and taking off his jacket.

-Kiss me, again, and much harder, please.

-Has Mark completely rejected you?

-Yes.

-You should hate him for that.

-I-

-Do.

-Only if you make love to me and satisfy me. Then, my hatred will be released.

-If you don't mind pain, I'll satisfy you. And, I'll hold you to that vow. We'll be allies.

-Then, do it!

Carmino took off his clothes and stood naked before her. Ramsay flung her own clothes carelessly onto the couch.

The pain was intense; but, its pleasure was almost unendurable. She wanted to cry out, but didn't dare. Carmino pinned her to the floor and rammed her mercilessly. His tongue reached into her mouth and his kisses were painful and so very pleasing like the sweet taste of the most subtle of poisons. His weapon seemed to lubricate her insides to an almost maddening degree of ecstasy.

-No!

-Yes, Ramsay.

He pulled out and sat on top of her.

-Run your tongue along this and please me!

She tasted the delicious weapon brimming with its milky essence. Carmino climaxed and forced Ramsay to gag on it. Then, he pushed her away and her head struck the floor. He got up and helped Ramsay to do the same. Neither one got dressed. Carmino lit two cigarettes and handed one to her.

-Take a deep puff and, then, put your clothes back on. Tell no one of this.

-Are you serious?

She laughed and threw her head back. Carmino grinned.

-Short, quick, and painful: the perfect sex, eh, Ramsay?

She exhaled the cigarette smoke in his face.

-Yes, as a matter of fact. You can put your pants back on, Carmino, it's not interesting anymore. Can I get you another drink?

-Scotch, please.

The door handle turned, accompanied by a loud knock.

-Ramsay?

Ramsay was not pleased at the sound of that voice. She dabbed on some lipstick and motioned for Carmino to take his drink. She unbolted the door.

-Why was this door locked?

-We needed privacy.

-"We?" And, who is this other person you're entertaining? There should be no one else here tonight.

Carmino came forward.

-Good evening, Julietta.

Julietta didn't look at him, but addressed herself to Ramsay.

-You have been entertaining. You should put a comb through your hair, my dear. Carmino, are you here to help us or to sabotage our efforts? I wonder.

Still, Julietta did not look at Carmino, who may have played an indirect role in her son's murder. With her clear and ancient eyes, she apprised her daughter-in-law who was now combing her hair. For all of Ramsay's beauty, Julietta felt her to be careless and even ruthless. The latter quality, she much admired. She switched off one of the two remaining lights. Darkness appealed to her, and she did not wish to be scrutinized by these two people.

Carmino lit another cigarette and offered one to Julietta. She ignored the offering and continued to address herself to Ramsay.

-Everything is in readiness. Mark has secluded himself downstairs, and he'll remain there until our arrival. I've prepared a tray of food for us in the kitchen; would you be so kind as to bring it in? It shouldn't be too heavy for you.

Ramsay left the room.

-Sit down, Carmino.

He sat down in the chair opposite the sofa which was the furthest point from where Julietta was sitting. He didn't like this woman.

-Well?

-I'm glad that you're here with us, tonight. It saves me the trouble of hunting you down for the animal that I know you to be. Do not interrupt me, Carmino!

-Go to hell.

-You amuse me, you fool; but, we need you here, tonight. We'll have to be burdened with you for still another eternity. How awful the price of balance. But, tell me, who was the traitor amongst us? Who informed the priests of the habits of our group? Tell me.

-I don't know. Contrary to your beliefs, I've never been in league with our enemies. Don't laugh at me!

-I shouldn't laugh at a man who takes me for a fool? Liar! Traitor! You've played both sides well, but not well enough.

-Filth!

-I shall remember that when my son is brought back to life.

-Remember it, Julietta.

Carmino's self-assurance wavered a bit at the mention of a formidable opponent. He was Jeffrey's inferior and he knew it. Although, the damage to his pride was minimal, Jeffrey's shadow still held weight upon him.

-Thinking, Carmino?

-Yes. I'm thinking.

-Share the thought.

-Two men and two women for this monumental moment. The priests have surrounded the house, you know. They're waiting for us to begin the ceremony.

-Go on, please.

-They plan to slaughter us.

-Including you; their friend and collaborator?

-I've never been their ally.

-An accomplice, then?

-Don't push me too far, Julietta.

-You bore me with your protests of innocence. How I despise you! However, you're needed.

-What will be our defense against the priests? A locked door won't do a damned bit of good.

-True. But, a sealed door will do much good. Offer me a cigarette, Carmino.

-Of course.

-Thank you.

Ramsay came back into the room carrying a tray of cakes and tea: all of it made from scratch by Julietta. Carefully, she set the tray down on to the coffee table.

-May I pour you a cup of tea?

-If you would, please. Are you not sitting nearer to Carmino?

Ramsay didn't answer.

-I'm waiting for your answer, Ramsay.

-Your tea.

-Thank you.

-Carmino?

-I'll help myself.

He took a cake with his tea. Ramsay noted that his eating habits were impeccable.

-When do we begin?

-"We?" Could you possibly be referring to your imagined participation in a ritual?

-Yes.

-Sometimes, I almost like you, Carmino. But, how can one like a person whom one can't trust?

-I'm sure I don't know.

-Humility? Do I detect it in your voice?

-Never humility, Julietta.

Ramsay listened with amusement to this interchange, grateful to be left out.

-Indeed? Your act of contrition tonight is a proof of your humility. You're here to beg participation.

-No.

-You will, Carmino. And, still, I may not have you.

-You will.

-I could easily turn you out.

-Ramsay wouldn't. Ramsay?

-I want Carmino to stay.

-Very well, he stays.

Julietta was not upset or even annoyed because it was the answer she had been expecting: an answer that had taken the decision and the irritation from her own hands...a carefully laid plan that had succeeded. Her enemy would now be close at hand.

-Should we prepare now? I've brought no magical weapons with me.

-Everything has been prepared by Marcus and me.

-Good. By the way, Julietta, the tea was delicious. I'm relieved that it wasn't poisoned.

CHAPTER XXII
RESURRECTION

OUTSIDE, IN the rain and the dark, beneath the shelter of an awning, stood a priest: a lone figure, at the moment, whose comrades were strategically fixed within the perimeter of the town house. The rain didn't diminish the smell of death and decay that hovered upon this priest for nothing could dispel that. The filthy globe of yellowish light was about him, as always.

This particular priest wanted immortality, and he wanted to be cleansed of that odor of death and to wash his hands of the blood which despoiled his soul -- not an easy task. When would the killings stop? Not tonight, surely. Tonight would culminate in more slaughters, but not his. He had to survive and board the solar boat and pass through the solar flame which did not consume the physical. Just a few more killings and it would be ended.

Renso's mind was demented and his soul was corrupt.

His fellow priests were worse.

Mark's hand touched the cold stone and his bare feet absorbed the warmth of the floor. On two sides of the temple stood the eight sarcophagi evenly spaced with the head facing toward the center point of the chamber. In the east was the altar and upon this were set the ankh, the scroll, the scarab, and the gold tube.

Time was short and Mark needed Julietta to begin the Mass. She would be priestess and he would be deacon. And, Carmino? Mark knew he was in the house. It would be a long and complex ritual and their focus could not waver for a moment. What were their chances for success? A good question; but, perhaps, its answer shouldn't be speculated upon for didn't that question imply doubt or even failure?

Mark ran his hand through his hair. He lit the two lamps and extinguished all other lights and, then, placed himself within an upright sarcophagus. He waited.

Renso walked through the pouring rain to join his comrades. His robe was soaked through. The color of his flesh was pallid and his eyes were vacuous and, yet, they were filled with a purpose. The other six priests gathered with him, and not too far away lay their slain comrades.

It was time for them to enter the house and learn the secrets of life and death.

Julietta allowed Ramsay and Carmino to enter the temple's chamber without her, while she waited outside the double doors. Carmino held back.

-Why do you hesitate, Carmino? Surely, fear is unknown to you.

-Not entirely, Julietta; it's good to keep fear as an emotion for preparation and counter- attack.

-Counter-attack? But, who has attacked you?

-I was referring to the future.

-The word has no meaning for me. I don't believe in your linear time scheme. I am the proof that it doesn't exist.

-Tell your watch dog in there to throw away his dagger.

-Indeed?

-Well?

-I will not. Face him, Carmino, and let the better man win.

Carmino shrugged his shoulders and smiled. He turned his lean form to face the entrance of the chamber. He walked in. Julietta shut the doors behind him and remained outside in deep thought.

-Soon, it will begin, and my son will be brought back to me. We gods will take our place in a new universe. How long I've waited and now the longest and most dreadful moment in this world's history will begin. For twelve thousand years, I have waited and wandered and kept myself hidden at all costs. For ten thousand of those years, I had to watch my beloved Sumer and Egypt slowly deteriorate into death worshipping cults. How horrible to witness it! I was born into the beautiful lands of the Tigris and Euphrates...a child of artificial birth by the hands of the ancient architects: the ancient dynasty of gods who set the world once more into motion to preserve it and to place the keys of civilization into its hands. They came from the unknown planet and, once again, aided us.

Julietta paused in her memories for a moment.

-Sumer flourished under their guidance and the arts and sciences were as one. For over three thousand years, civilization was sustained and even the hand of progress could be felt; air vehicles and electricity were not unknown to us. And, then, they left us...and the decline began. Unrest and civil war divided the great land until my son, our Pharaoh, reunited his mighty and sacred land. The so-called beginning of recorded history began: an art that is now taken so literally. Sumer will once again flourish, but it will be under the ordered law that Rome once founded: an empire that I am still quite fond of...such order and sanitation, and their roads were quite splendid, too. They did well.

Carmino took his place to the side of the flame-lit chamber and made himself reasonably comfortable on the stone floor. He took off his shoes and socks and assumed a semi-lotus position. Silently, he chanted his mantra and thought...

-Dear Jeffrey, we will soon meet, again. You will see your father and greet him with a kiss. Will Ramsay betray me to you? I think not. Interesting...she's still wearing her high heels, and no ritual garment. It may just work out.

Carmino kept staring at Ramsay and gained a certain amount of solace from her femininity. He drew comfort from her, even though it was not her intention to give comfort. Her thoughts were not involved with his at the moment as well they shouldn't be.

Carmino thought about his past. After the birth of his son, he had receded into the scattered outlines of history and historical figures; always there, his hand, his voice and manipulations were felt, but his presence never seen. He had guided his son for his four hundred year reign upon the throne of Egypt, and well he advised that son to "die" and pass the scepter to his own heir; each heir's lifetime growing shorter and inferior. Slowly, the empire collapsed into decay. The greatness that once was became pathetic pantomime, and disciplined cruelty gave way to softness and the entrance into their country of inferiors... rabble.

The great monuments withstood the tenacity of time and the elemental onslaught while the inferior structures crumbled to dust. The bloodline was interrupted and only once did Carmino take an active role in his country's history: an unwritten event later to be documented by scribes with much of the truth missing from the tale. An upstart who had proclaimed himself as "chosen" to lead his people from Egypt had appeared. A battle of magicians was waged, and it was through an almost imperceptible mistake on Carmino's part that he had been defeated and his only son nearly killed. The plague had been set into motion and its effect was deadly. It was only through chance...a mishap...a shifting of the winds and no more... nevertheless, Carmino had been defeated.

-Are you ready to begin, Carmino?

-Yes.

-Your mind seemed so far away. Do you need a few moments?

-No, thank you, Ramsay. Let's begin, and get Julietta in here to seal us up.

Ramsay knew that the priests had entered the house and were now on their way to the chamber. She went to the double doors and opened them. Julietta came in and closed the doors behind her, affixing a sacred wax seal to the center. Ramsay and Carmino breathed a sigh of relief for if that seal were broken, the penalty would be exacting. For the moment, they were safe from violation.

Ramsay began the ritual with the priests outside listening.

-Hear my pray. Great ones, I implore you to aid your daughter in this dreaded operation to defy those laws of Man and gods. Give to us the means in which to carry forth our work. Proclaim us as worthy.

The air became charged with diffuse light and sound, rendering it impossible to see anything with clarity. Ramsay was surprised at how quickly the air had transformed itself, and so was Carmino. He was impressed. Julietta had expected nothing less from her daughter-in- law; and it was she who now knelt before the altar uplifting her arms toward the heavens.

-Hear your creation and speak to us who are gathered here in this chamber. We seek to raise our dead.

Ramsay came forward and knelt next to Julietta and spoke.

-Great one, guide my hand and words and place within my body the sound of life. Your sons and daughters are here, but they need the pull of the silver chord to bring them once more to the physical plane. Can I say no more and no less? If I am unworthy, then take my life and I will accept that fate.

The air became more hazy as the people in the chamber heard voices...voices of the gods who had descended from the skies thousands of years ago. The voices were a murmur, but Ramsay, Julietta, and Carmino listened. Mark listened and prayed within his stone coffin.

The two women stood up and approached the main altar stone and took from it the sacred objects. Ramsay held the gold tube and ankh while Julietta held the scarab and the scroll. It was Julietta who walked toward Mark's coffin.

-Enter this temple.

Mark emerged from his coffin and Julietta placed the scroll in his hand. Together, they walked back to where Ramsay stood. The three of them faced each other to form the triangle. Ramsay led the way toward Jeffrey's coffin. She affixed the ankh's point at the head of the coffin and commanded Mark to push the lid open. Quickly! Mark did as commanded and the body was exposed to the temple's charged air. Ramsay caught her breath at the sight of the man who was perfectly preserved; his eyes were open and fixed upon her.

Ramsay touched the ankh to the center of Jeffrey's forehead. Julietta placed the scarab on his breast and Mark unrolled the papyrus sheet. Ramsay glanced back at her priest who nodded that he was ready. For a moment, she hesitated from fright. The emotion passed and she knelt down beside the sarcophagus. She leaned over to place the gold cylinder to the ear of her husband. Mark read from the scroll of life and death, and Ramsay repeated his words.

-Hear me and command my voice. Ra, place your burning hand upon the heart of your son. Infuse in him your radiant light and warmth and, once again, imprison his soul within the flesh of your flesh.

A horrible silence followed. Ramsay almost uttered a cry of despair. Carmino came and stood beside her.

-Continue, Ramsay.

-Ra, we stand in your house and will soon be taken into the heart of your heart. Re- animate the soul within the frame of this body. Look into the eyes of your son and let him return your gaze, Father of us all. The wind of the heavens that stirs the planet and carries your precious vibration to every living entity. The wind that stirs the waters of the great seas and casts the waves upon the shore. The wind that guides the stars and wandering bodies upon the heavens. Touch this man's breast! Stir the heart and cast the wind into his eyes to shed tears of sorrow and joy!

Did Jeffrey's eyes flicker? Ramsay's heart pounded in her chest as her body became soaked with sweat. Her hand trembled, and she had to take a firm grasp on the gold cylinder. Jeffrey's hands reached up to touch his wife's face. She looked at him with mixed emotions.

Carmino spoke.

-Finish the reading, Mark.

-Fire, the element that is and is not; it crosses the threshold of the barrier which separates your kingdom from our mortal plane. It gives life and death and is the purity of both those beloved gifts. Its tongues are the delicious waves of warmth and heat and still it may not be touched by the profane! Breathe it into the body of your son!

Jeffrey sat up in his coffin and took Ramsay's hand. And, then, blackness took hold of the room...it was plunged into the black abyss of change and death and new beginnings. One couldn't see his hand before his face, and even the two flaming torches were like dying stars. It was unsettling, and all of those with life in the chamber held out their arms for unseen support.

-Remain calm and continue the ceremony. I must speak to my wife. Mother, take Ramsay's place. Carmino and Mark, you will both continue and no blood is to be shed between the two of you.

Jeffrey removed the scarab from his breast and placed it in Julietta's hand as if he could see the woman in the depths of blackness. Ramsay had to hand Julietta the ankh and, somehow, she managed to do it. But, how would Mark read from his scroll?

-Ramsay, the cylinder?

-I can't see you, Mark.

-There! I have it. Now, help Jeffrey to emerge.

Jeffrey leaned on Ramsay's shoulder and together they extricated him from his resting place. It was then that Ramsay caught sight of two eyes shining in the dark. It was Osiris. It was comforting to be able to see the cat. Jeffrey and Ramsay made their way to the double door. They leaned against it while in the background could be heard the muffled voices of Mark and Julietta.

-Ramsay, was it you who betrayed us and opened the doors to the priests?

-You don't waste any time, do you? No.

-A direct and simple answer is the proof of your maturity.

-Not a very flattering question to ask your wife. Will you ask it of the others?

The question was pointed and it contained an interrogative within itself. Jeffrey grasped the implication as he steadied himself against the doors. His hand touched the wax seal.

-There are priests behind this barrier. Why have they been allowed to gain such close proximity?

-Avoiding my question, Jeffrey?

-I was asking one of my own.

-Answer mine first. I'm not so sure I can answer yours.

-I'll ask the remaining seven the same question that I've just asked you.

-Oh? I take it you're not asking Julietta or Mark and not even Carmino? Interesting.

-My mother is above suspicion.

-Placed there by you? How typical of a devoted son. Anyway, I expected that, and I can almost respect your loyalty to blood. It's not so bad.

-Thank you for the left-handed compliment. Look, Allyson rises...and how beautiful she looks.

-You can see her? I can't see anything.

-I have the eyes of a cat. And, now, my dear, an answer to my question.

-I don't know. I- I wasn't thinking. Are we trapped in here now?

-That would appear to be the case; but, there may be other means of escape.

-Is Mark also above suspicion?

-Yes.

-I won't pursue that.

Jeffrey saw the smile on Ramsay's face and the arch of her eyebrow. He felt no shame in loving another man.

-And, Carmino?

-In his own way, he, too, is above reproach. My father is a good chess player and knows how to advance his moves. He's a master of deception; but, not a traitor.

-Good for him.

-You admire him. How have you kept yourself these past years, Ramsay?

-You don't know? I thought that you would come back knowing everything.

-I've come back exactly as I was for there is no progression on the other side of this mantle. I come back in full consciousness and that is the advantage.

-What is it like? I'm almost afraid to ask.

-Difficult to describe...the vision is different: one sees everything as within a circle of motion. The awareness is greatly heightened, but now it's slipping from my memory as we speak. One sees no thing in particular, but the sense of the essence is-

-Yes? Go on!

-The priests are waiting for us.

-How can we escape?

-Let the others rise to their feet and, then, I'll speak to them.

-But, please continue your story, Jeffrey-

-Not now. Close your eyes and allow me to pass my hand over your forehead. You must have a vision and this vision must be told to me in all its detail. Close your eyes, Ramsay, and listen only to the sound of my voice. Be at one with me for I am your guide and your master. Listen to me! Hear me and speak from your soul.

Ramsay closed her eyes and felt the soothing hand of Jeffrey pass over her forehead. The sensation was but a moment; but, the moment seemed a dream's eternity. Another part of Ramsay was now in an old dimension that had once been called a universe by a forgotten race of souls. She stood upon a pavement of stone within the wall of a doomed city...a doomed universe. The eerie silence of dread was overwhelming. The god who presided over this stillness was a dreaded god whose many lifetimes had carried him to the abyss of despair and blackness; so many incarnations for a few silent moments. The price of immortality was not to be trifled with.

These thoughts passed through Ramsay's mind as she opened her eyes and gazed about this world. The air was of a reddish hue and there were great spurts of flame everywhere. The streets were strewn with rocks and debris. Many buildings were still intact, but all of them had the air of death; no breeze stirred and no coolness could be felt.

Ramsay looked toward the sky and gasped. The vault of heaven seemed suspended just above her head. Instinctively, she put her arm out to stop it from hitting her, but it remained above, suspended by a thread that would soon snap...a thread that had to give way.

She turned away from it and began walking down the remains of a street, carefully picking her way through the stone and the scattered rocks. Ramsay looked into the distance and saw the silhouettes of people walking toward her. The silhouettes soon cleared themselves into images of people whom she recognized. They approached her.

-My name is Ramsay Bast.

-We know who you are and what you are soon to become. We are on that point of evolution toward that state which will bring us to the cause of all. Our journey toward the great wall of separation will soon begin. Do you understand, Ramsay?

-No. But, perhaps, my soul does...explain it to me. An account of this is expected of me, and I don't want to disappoint my husband and my friends.

-The solar boat will soon come for us and we will evolve into the gods of your scriptures.

-The god of Sumer and Egypt?

-In a manner of speaking. Soon, the solar boat will come for you, and you must be ready to accept your immortality. Your soul will be expected to evolve without the benefit of incarnations; it is a privilege that you will no longer be in need of. You and your friends will be the gods of the next universe.

-By whose decree?

-There is a traitor amongst you. Listen to me as I whisper the name.

Explosions broke out and flames shot through the crevices of the pavement. The ceiling of heaven began to descend.

-We must go now.

Ramsay looked up and saw a disc of brilliance cut its way through the descending mass of stars. It looked like a brilliant gem stone gracefully coming toward them. She could not bear to look at it. Ramsay closed her eyes and once again felt Jeffrey's cooling touch upon her forehead.

-Are you all right, Ramsay?

-I think so Jeffrey. I must tell you-

-Point out the traitor to me. All of our comrades have arisen and they await us.

-And, the priests; are they waiting for us also?

-One of them must replace the traitor in our midst. One can come to terms with a known quantity and, perhaps, even temper that quality.

-I don't share your belief; but, I won't argue with you just now.

-The traitor?

-Give me the torch and I'll point her out to you.

Jeffrey took one of the two torches from its holder and placed it in Ramsay's hand.

-Do your deed, my dear.

The others were gathered in a circle just a few feet from them. Ramsay didn't hesitate in her task for a suspicion that had long lingered in her mind had been confirmed: a fragment of a woman's sentence now repeated itself to her, "...their foul smell of death." She couldn't help but grin at this clue which had been dropped at her feet so many years ago.

Ramsay's torch illuminated faces: how wonderful to see them! Allyson, Armando, her dear Aunt Francesca, Timothy and Kenjiro, she smiled at her friends. Lisa looked up at her with a startled look.

-Dear Ramsay-

-You're the traitor.

Ramsay pointed the torch at Tana.

-I don't know what you are talking about. How dare you! Do you hear what your wife is accusing me of Jeffrey? Stop her!

-Why, Tana?

-It's a monstrous lie. Jeffrey, you cannot believe this of me. I implore you-

-Why, Tana?

-I tell you it is not true!

Tana's voice was brittle in timber. Her body quavered on the point of convulsion.

Carmino stepped forward.

-Admit your treachery and your death will be quick, but not merciful. You must suffer pain.

-No! Please...I beg of you! I was frightened. I didn't want to die, and they betrayed me, as well.

-You fool! You awful fool! I feel no pity for you.

-You cannot kill me, Carmino. The number must be twelve. You cannot replace me with so little time left.

Carmino grabbed the torch from Ramsay's hand.

-A cleansing fire should purge you, darling.

-No! Jeffrey, stop him!

Carmino set the torch to Tana's clothes. In an instant, she was a burning mass of flame which Carmino manipulated without mercy: a dispassionate executioner who went about his task. He kept the burning mass contained to one quadrant of the chamber: the quadrant of fire and consumption. Tana's death screams were awful to hear; but, with the exception of Allyson, who cried in Mark's arms, all remained unaffected.

CHAPTER XXIII
THE NEW GODS

CARMINO SLAMMED shut the lid of the sarcophagus.

-Jeffrey, is there a safe way out of here?

-A long time ago, Carmino, Mark and I installed a false bottom into my coffin; from there, we can descend down a flight of stairs and into a passage that will lead us directly into the garden. However, we must first lay a death trap for our friends.

-But, one of them must be allowed to escape with us, no?

-We must take our leave first, Francesca. Mark, you and I will wait at the bottom of the staircase and allow one of the wretches to pass to safety. Julietta, break the seal.

-Just give me the signal.

Mark was now at the sarcophagus where Jeffrey had been interred for the past thirty years. He climbed into it and knelt down to feel for the mechanism which would release the trap door. It was difficult to locate. Carmino brought the torch over to bear on the darkness within the stone coffin. Osiris jumped into the coffin and flicked at the metal loop with his paw. Mark pulled the metal rung and the trap door flung open. Carmino beckoned them to come forward one at a time.

Jeffrey signaled Julietta to break the wax seal. She did so, removing the wax inscription and releasing the magical binding that she had affixed to the double doors. She joined the others and soon they were all beneath the ritual chamber.

Mark and Jeffrey remained at the foot of the staircase while the others made their way into the dark passage which would take them to the relative safety of the garden.

-I hear them, Jeffrey. They've entered the chamber.

The priests were making their way into the chamber with daggers poised to kill. They knew that it had been too easy to break the doors' seal and...there was the smell of burnt flesh. Their morbid curiosity led them to Tana's coffin.

-Pray that one comes to this coffin, Mark.

-I will.

Their prayers were answered at their moment of request. The lone priest, Renso, had chanced to gaze into the coffin and had seen an outline of blackness within its dark confines. He stepped in to have a look and fell feet first down the stairs.

-Got him! Mark, push the door up and bolt it into place. I'll take care of our friend here.

-I will not struggle for I intended to come with you. How will you kill my brothers?

-Don't ask what doesn't concern you.

Jeffrey was feeling along the stone wall for a lever...once found, he gently pushed it in. And, then, still one more lever... The screams from above could be heard. The oil had been released and the remaining torch which had been put back into place by Ramsay had been let loose from its holder and dropped to the floor. Death by fire was horrible for it burned the very air that one breathed and, yet, one still lived for a brief, agonizing time.

Jeffrey, Mark, and Renso soon found themselves in the breezy air of the garden. It was surrounded by a high wall and, at this time of season, the flowers and trees were in full bloom. It had stopped raining.

Jeffrey spoke.

-Very soon, the end will come. Look at the night sky. Does it look more brilliant, more radiant, than ever?

Indeed, the infinite roof above their heads appeared brilliant with the stars of the galaxy. Even the white, translucent gauze of the Milky Way seemed to weave its way around the earth and the moon: a full moon with an aura about it which pulsated and touched the air of its sister planet.

Jeffrey pointed to the sky.

-Look! The stars and constellations appear to be lost within each other's sphere of influence. The night is a brilliant star pulsating into a unity never before witnessed by a mortal being. Soon, there will be no more constellations or galaxies only a pure thought of light which will rent a hole through this confinement that was called a universe and emerge into the nothingness of eternity that will form the foundation of time and space in the new dawn of a new beginning: a universe from out of this black hole!

All about them, the heavens converged. The vault of the sky became a glowing mass of white stars and galaxies merging into each other. The moon's outline was quickly lost against this newly created night sky. Space and time and matter were now converging upon each other.

The twelve people and Osiris knelt in the garden as the white light flickered over them: a cold radiance, that would soon turn to heat, bathed the planet. In moments, all physical life would cease and the souls released would take their places within the heavens that were now descending upon them.

A point of light released itself from the sky and descended: a perfectly shaped disc of brilliant substance. In the thought of a moment, it hovered above the twelve people and cat and lifted them into its protection. Their bodies fused within it and the solar boat thrust its way toward the fiery orb known to mankind as the sun.

The solar disc penetrated the outer layer visible to Man. Its journey took it into the heart of that radiant orb as the rest of the universe collapsed in upon the fire god. Eternities passed within eternities as the solar disc dove into the heart of radiance. Light beget light and the blinding brilliance of solar matter rippled past and through the solar boat: the liquid fire that is substance to gods...liquid, white fire that coursed over the brilliant solar vehicle in streams of endless light.

The purest thought was again being formed and compressed into a pinpoint of light against the black nothingness which cannot be conceived of by human minds. This pinpoint of light contained the disc...the gods of a new universe...renting a hole through the black veil of the black abyss. It would emerge intact into the formless and the timeless. The disc would be released and the explosion of the light would commence. A line would be drawn across nothingness in the trail of the gods' vehicle and, then, the triangle of manifestation would commence...as it must! The pure thought would nova and give birth to the dimensions of time and space: an almost infinite universe freed from the black hole of confinement. The thirteen new gods bore witness to it all. The event was witnessed and recorded.

The solar disc of the gods circled in endless night about the newly forming universe until the firmament was formed under the aegis of the first star; and, then, the disc settled upon the planet and the gods emerged. They waited for the dawn. These gods stood upon the great barren plain of the first planet. They caused their vehicle to stand upon itself: a new monument which vibrated the celestial and dreaded knowledge of the cause. The pinnacles of art and intelligence were contained within the vibrating disc...the skyscraper of heaven.

The sacred structures would be built with the power of thought and awareness. These edifices would not crumble. They would be the birth place of Man and this planet would be the center of the new universe.

The new dynasty stood upon the plain.

Ramsay and Jeffrey: the leaders.

Julietta and Carmino: the ancient mother and father.

Allyson and Mark: the lovers.

Timothy and Francesca: the soothsayers.

Armando and Lisa: the bearers of culture and art.

Kenjiro and Renso: the warrior and his student.

Osiris: giver of wisdom.

They focused their minds and began the architecture of their new realm.

The first day in the new universe had begun.

The End

APPENDIX

RAMSAY'S DECK OF CARDS:

THE ICE QUEEN: of beauty and coldness. A reflection on one's self image in a moment of forever.

MATADOR OF BLOOD: a young and handsome man who sheds the blood of the beast or is it his own blood that is shed?

THE PHYSICIAN: the healer of life and, therefore, the taker. A man not to be entirely trusted.

THE HOUSE OF NO DOORS AND WINDOWS: an inescapable prison within one's own mind. The release is in the end of a dream or death.

THE PRIEST: neither good nor bad...he is as severe as death or as enigmatic as a dream.

THE PRIEST OF DREAD: an enemy to everyone.

THE PRIEST OF DECEIT: a hidden enemy.

THE PRIEST OF DECAY: the loss of self and the good within.

THE PRIEST OF LOVE AND DEATH: a hidden lover.

THE PRIESTESS: the woman of no compromise. The ruler and the ruled.

THE PRIESTESS OF DREAD: an enemy.

THE PRIESTESS OF DECEIT: a recognized enemy who goes unrecognized.

THE PRIESTESS OF DECAY: debauchery.

THE DEACON: a young man or woman who is easily lead astray and, yet, this person can be strong depending on the surrounding cards.

THE PHANTOM OF RECOLLECTION: remembrance of fragmented dreams.

THE BLANK CARD: the end of a life.

THE CROSSROADS OF INFINITY: the last and most important decision that a mortal will ever make.

LIGHTNING AND THUNDER: precursors of an event or the culmination of one...proceed with great caution for one misstep can lead to annihilation.

CAT AND MOUSE: a hunter and the hunted...the latter usually having no choice or chance.

KILLER BLADE: a death that is swift and brought about by one's own hand or taken upon an enemy. It is the supreme act of courage.

SAMURAI: strength, agility, courage...fearlessness and ruthlessness.

SAMURAI: THE EDGE OF A DREAM: an awakening and a realization that is not always pleasant.

THE HANGED MAN: courage in the face of any danger.

SHATTERED GLASS: past lives exposed and the memories of this life resurrected.

THE TOWER OF THE ELEMENTALS: a perspective that is doomed and, yet, a new path is opened to meet at the crossroads of infinity: confusion and chaos.

MAN OF FORTUNE AND MISFORTUNE: duplicity which can be to one`s advantage or disadvantage..

MAN OF DESTINY: meeting your holy guardian angel whom you may not like.

FUN AND GAMES: treachery and deliberate cruelty.

THE MIRROR: a reflection into a parallel life.

THE LEADER: a mature and intelligent man or woman of courage and initiative.

THE LOVERS: fidelity and protection.

THE STUDENT: learned, ignorant, and impressionable.

THE SOOTHSAYER: a clairvoyant who is never wrong.

THE GIVER OF ART AND WISDOM: the builder of civilization.

THE WARRIOR: an aggressor who suffers not the weak.

THE MOTHER: giver of life and mortality

THE FATHER: the originator of the universe.

ABOUT THE AUTHOR

Gerard Denza has worked in the Publicity Dept. at Random House and Little, Brown, and Co. in New York City. He's worked with such authors as Pete Hamill, Arthur C. Clarke, Willie Morris, Pat Booth, and Kevin and Todd Berger. He's the author and director of six Off-Off Broadway plays that include: ICARUS, MAHLER: THE MAN WHO WAS NEVER BORN, THE DYING GOD: A VAMPIRE'S TALE, SHADOWS BEHIND THE FOOTLIGHTS, and THE HOUSEDRESS. HIs noir play, EDMUND: THE LIKELY, has been recorded for radio broadcast.

Mr. Denza is a graduate of Fordham University at Lincoln Center where he majored in psychology.

He can be contacted at gerarddenza.com,

He lives in New York City where he is hard at work on his next novel: THE IMMORTAL: AN EDWARD MENDEZ, P. I. THRILLER.